A Spectre is Haunting Greentree

Carson Winter

Cover Art by Stefan Koidl
Interior Illustrations by Matt Blairstone
Edited by Alex Woodroe

Content warnings are available at the end of this book. Please consult this list for any particular subject matter you may be sensitive to.

TENEBROUS

PRESS

Published by Tenebrous Press.
Visit our website at www.tenebrouspress.com.

Production of this novel was made possible in part by a grant from the Regional Arts & Culture Council. Visit https://racc.org/ for more information.

First Printing, August 2024.

Print ISBN: 978-1-959790-04-4
eBook ISBN: 978-1-959790-05-1

Cover art by Stefan Koidl.

Interior illustrations by Matt Blairstone.

Edited by Alex Woodroe.

Formatting by Lori Michelle.

Selected Works from Tenebrous Press:

From the Belly
a novel by Emmett Nahil

Mouth
a novella by Joshua Hull

Lumberjack
a novella by Anthony Engebretson

Posthaste Manor
a novel by Jolie Toomajan & Carson Winter

The Black Lord
a novella by Colin Hinckley

Dehiscent
a novella by Ashley Deng

House of Rot
a novella by Danger Slater

Agony's Lodestone
a novella by Laura Keating

Soft Targets
a novella by Carson Winter

Crom Cruach
a novella by Valkyrie Loughcrewe

Lure
a novella by Tim McGregor

One Hand to Hold, One Hand to Carve
a novella by M.Shaw

More titles at www.TenebrousPress.com

To my fellow worriers.

CHAPTER ONE

HER HEART CLENCHED like a fist.

She fell to one knee, then to the other. The other shoppers, who just moments before had been oblivious, took notice. They stopped and stared at the woman who held her chest, hyperventilating. Carina swiveled her head wildly looking for help. She couldn't breathe. She was gasping and tears ran down her cheeks. With some effort, she managed, "Help me."

Another woman came to her first; she put her hand on Carina's back. She said something Carina couldn't hear, but assumed was some sort of medical-adjacent pedigree. *I'm a nurse, or I'm a dental assistant, or I'm a med student, or—*

Carina's heart thumped in her chest to the rhythm of a horse race.

The Impromptu Medic felt for her pulse and soon, other people were standing by, craning for a look at the woman who fell down in the supermarket. Their eyes disrobed her. They drilled into her insides and she felt utterly and completely transparent.

"Somebody call an ambulance," said Ms. Medic.

Three or four people reached for their phones, all placing the same call in the same manner. "Yes, I'm at the Grab-N-Go on Fifth. A woman is having trouble breathing, she's grabbing at her chest. No, no, I don't know her. About forty, maybe. Maybe forty-five. Excuse me, ma'am, how old are you?"

Carina closed her eyes tight and all she could hear was the relentless, insistent tempo of her heart. It was a hummingbird, a piston, a drumroll into forever. Carina was sure she would die in a supermarket, surrounded by faces painted with concerned curiosity. She would die a show. She kept breathing, shoveling air like it was coal into the furnace of the Titanic. Carina was sinking.

She was dying. Everyone was talking and she was going to die and soon new voices joined the fray and the stimulation made Carina want to shake off her own skin and just run and hide like a sick pet ready to perish with grace. She tried to scream but she just let out a low raspy gasp and when she opened her eyes, she saw new faces, young faces.

"Are you having trouble breathing?"

The question didn't register at first. She tried to explain: *no, I'm dying*, but the blandly courteous face of the EMT made her reconsider. *Maybe I'm not dying*, she thought. *Or maybe I'm already dead and this is what an angel looks like. Hello, angel, lovely to meet you.*

"Yes," she said finally, hedging her bets.

"Heart's really kicking here," he said.

Yes, it was flipping and kicking and thumping and drumming—

"Are you feeling any pressure, like an elephant sitting on your chest?"

Carina shook her head. *No,* she thought but couldn't say, *but I'm so fucking scared.*

The young man who was connecting wires to her chest frowned. "Alrighty then," he said lightly. "I think you're okay, but it'll be good to get someone else to look at you."

Hospital! It's happening, I'm gone. I'm going to die. All because I saw him.

They spoke to her softly, in controlled tones. They reassured her, told her everything would be fine. The bystanders clapped when they put her on the stretcher. They cheered when she was swallowed by the ambulance. Tears streamed down her cheeks as humiliation and terror commingled in her chest, where her heartbeat was slowly steadying to a normal, fretful pace.

"You'll be okay," they said. "We'll make sure of it."

She kept her eyes closed though. She didn't want to risk seeing him again.

(*Even if it wasn't him, even if it wasn't anyone.*)

One of the EMTs held her hand. "Probably just a panic attack," he said. "Happens more than you think."

In the hospital, where she waited for her release papers—after a bored doctor told her that there was nothing wrong with her—she felt waves of adrenaline jolt her heart every time a dark-haired attendant walked past her room. Each time, with his head turned, she thought frantically: *It's him again, it's him!* But then, he would turn his head, and it would not be Steve and she would sigh and her self-loathing would blossom anew.

In her apartment, in the Baltimore suburbs, in her room with closed blinds and her laptop, in the white-light of her monitor, she typed.

Hey Em,

How's life out West?

She blinked under the light and pressed send, already waiting for a response. It was an invitation to be saved.

Eventually, it came.

Carina nodded at the reply, as if Emily were right there beside her, looking at her with those sharp green eyes and killer eyeliner, trim and elegant; a mom, a career woman, domestic to a fault. Emily contained multitudes. Carina often saw herself as younger than Emily, despite being the same age. She would find herself thinking, *One day, I'll have my shit together.*

A tremor formed in her throat.

Am I really doing this?

It's the right move, she thought. *It's the safe move.*

Then: *I'm a beggar. I'm begging right now.*

Carina breathed, just like the doctor told her to.

Her heart leapt at the creak of a floorboard.

Outside, a footstep.

On the other side of the door, down the hallway—there was the Great Unknowable *Someone.*

She held her breath.

She counted to ten.

One, two, three, four . . .

She exhaled.

"Nothing," she said to no one. "You're being silly." And then, when she could assure herself of only the most absolute silence, she began to pack.

Chapter Two

"ONE BOURBON, MARY," he said.

Steve Calico sidled up to the bar and the woman who was young enough to be his daughter wriggled her nose in unconscious discomfort. He watched her pour the drink, giving him one of those weak, slightly nauseous smiles. One of those professional, go-fuck-yourself smiles. *This how they treat regulars here?*

But, he controlled himself.

He read her distaste like a book. *Stuck-up. Bitch. Whore.*

But still, he did nothing.

He craned his neck and looked around the bar. It was mostly empty except for a couple old timers who sat drinking wine and reading newspapers under neon signs. The others, the ones like him, the boys, would be over soon, and with them would come some semblance of belonging.

Steve Calico didn't like to admit it, but alone, he was not nearly the man he pretended to be. The bartender served him another bourbon, this time with a more fixed expression, more decidedly pleasant. If the boys were here, he'd tell her what he really thought of her, what he'd do to wipe that smile off her face.

But Steve was alone, so he did nothing but sit and stir and drink.

It wasn't long before he felt a familiar hand on his shoulder and a loud, greeting yelp. Bruce, with his long goatee and biker get-up; Freddy with his bone-thin frame and meth teeth. They stood as an odd pairing, one massive and burly, one waifish and soft. The boys had dwindled in numbers from four to two.

Steve furrowed his brow. "Where's the rest of them?"

"Couldn't make it," said Bruce. He combed his long, thinning hair behind one of his ears. "Carl's holed up with some bitch in

God-knows-where. Jack says he's got to work since they're bleeding him dry with child support."

Steve huffed. He was trying to keep his temper. He managed, mildly, "They couldn't make it out for one goddamn night?"

"Sorry, man," said Bruce. "Never know with those guys."

All the muscles in Steve's body tightened. For a moment, he felt as if his body were made of steel. He grinded his teeth. His fingers flexed around the glass.

Freddy fidgeted with his fingers. "Let's grab some beers, man. Yeah, yeah. Let's play some pool."

"Okay. Yeah. Sounds good."

Steve felt better the more he drank. His attitude improved with every sunk pocket, although he couldn't help but let his eyes wander to the door every time it opened.

Fwoosh.

Just another regular. Calm down, Steve-O. You're just a little jumpy.

They played five games, pickling themselves with booze until their words slurred.

Freddy stumbled to the side of the table, his cheeks rosy and his thin, brown hair matted to his sweating brow. He lined up his shot, then fell forward, laughing hysterically as his legs buckled.

Bruce howled, the crow's feet around his eyes tightening into claw marks. He crouched down and slapped his knee and Steve should've been angry, he should've been real pissed, because Freddy had fucked everything up, but for some reason, he just waved it away, his eyes half-closed, humming along to whatever country song played through the bar's speakers.

"Freddy's a fucking lightweight," laughed Bruce, half to himself. "A wonder how, with all the shit he pumps into his body."

Steve chuckled at that, but his eyes were still closed.

Freddy stood back up. He held the pool table for support. He was laughing with them, too loud and out of time, as the moment had already started to pass. When Steve and Bruce had moved on from the hilarity, Freddy was still laughing, now even harder. His mouth was stretched in a fixed yawn, his yellowjacket teeth lined like tombstones around the void of his maw. His eyes were slits now. Every few seconds, he'd fall back to the table and try to breathe again, a long huffing breath.

Steve didn't even see it coming, not really. They were just goofing off. Him and the boys, just like the old days. But then, there it was, out of nowhere:

The *voice*. "I think it's time for you to leave."

Steve and Bruce turned their heads.

The bartender, the pretty one who looked at Steve as if he were shit, was standing behind them, carefully out of reach.

Steve turned slow, slower than he would've turned if he weren't so drunk. "Who do you think you . . . "

"You're cut off. Time to leave." She tried to make it sound light and airy. More of an admonishing mother than a scared woman, but Steve smelled the blood in the water.

He pushed himself off the wall and took a step forward. "Who are you calling drunk?'

Behind him, Bruce was helping Freddy up, dusting him off, setting him on steady feet as if he were a top heavy GI Joe. "Get her, Steve. Show her what you're made of."

"Yeah," said Freddy, his voice raspy. "He's single now, you know?"

"You need to take a step back," she said, her voice barely shaking at all.

Steve shrugged, moving forward fluidly. He moved like the liquid that filled him. "And?"

She retreated a step. "Nestor! Nestor!"

Fwoosh.

Steve reached into his pocket. "We'll leave," he said. "I just want to show you something."

But before he could pull out his phone, his body jerked up off the ground.

Steve could smell the bouncer's cologne. It filled his lungs.

The moment he was in the air felt like an eternity. *Good thing I'm drunk*, he thought. *Or else this will really—*

He felt the wetness before he felt the impact. Cold beer, casually spilled through hours of pool, seeped through his clothing. He groaned as he felt the impact in his bones, however muted by drink.

Bruce and Freddy were staring down at him, their faces slack.

Beside the woman was the bouncer, a big motherfucker with a braid that went down his back. "Y'all need to leave," he said. "Now."

It was Steve's turn to stand on uneven legs. "I just wanted to show her a picture," he said, smiling. He was turning it on. Showing that he could be chill, charismatic when he wanted to. "I'm not trying to hurt anyone. I'm a nice guy, promise."

The bouncer turned to the bartender. "You alright, Mary?"

She nodded. To Steve, sharper, firmer: "You guys are wasted. You gotta leave."

He smiled broader. "Hey, let's not be rash. We're just having a good time here, nothin' bad is happening. Our friend just fell. And I just wanted to show you a picture."

Bruce and Freddy hollered behind him. "Show 'er, Steve!"

"You take one more step toward her an' I'm going to break your fucking neck, *hombre*."

Steve put up both of his hands, as if he were talking to police. "We'll leave peacefully, *amigo*. Promise. Just give me this and we'll leave." He reached into his pocket. "You see, I've had to deal with women all my life. Hot women, ugly women, old women, young women—if there's a woman out there, God knows I've dealt with her." He swiped through his phone. "Ah, there we go. We're all here because we're celebrating being done with one particular woman."

He held the phone toward her face. The bouncer started toward him.

"Not a promise, not a threat," said Steve, who was smiling and red in the face. "Just a fact. This is what happens to particular women."

On his phone was a face, black and blue and swollen to the point that it looked barely human. Bloody abrasions worked like cross hatching down the side of her face. Her eyes were swollen shut.

"You gotta get out of here, now."

Steve took a step back, and laughed. He turned to his friends, who wore the same cruel smile. "Alright, partner," he said. "We're gone."

Chapter Three

Carina always listened before leaving her apartment. She put her ear to the door and held her breath. She counted for ten seconds. She watched for breaks in the light that seeped under her door. All of these things were now small trials in her life, ever since she left Steve Calico.

In all honesty, she didn't mind that he lived his own life and stayed away from her, she minded that she couldn't stop seeing him everywhere she went.

She went to a new grocery store now, one where she hadn't had a panic attack in front of a hundred strangers. The memory of her gasping, confused, while onlookers watched with pity and urgent idleness sent chills of cringing sorrow through her spine. Carina wished very much for that part of her life to be burned out of her, to be stricken from the record in void-black ink.

But she knew she would live with that moment until the day she died. Just as she lived with the constant terror of Steve coming home from work; walking on eggshells as he cursed alone, demeaning her in public or in his most vicious moments—hitting her. He only did that when he was particularly out of sorts, when something else was bothering him, but after ten years of excruciating, routine trauma, Carina saw Emily and something clicked.

Emily was a college friend. In school, they both studied art, and when Carina left to get married to Steve in an unsuccessful attempt to start a family, Emily graduated and went on to teach high school kids art history and painting. Carina envied Emily in almost every way, but over the years remained correspondent.

It was during a rare meeting—two months prior to her public breakdown—that Carina decided to leave Steve.

Emily was in town, just for a day—a pit stop on the way to New York. Her lips were bright red, candy apple like an old Mustang, and Carina herself could barely speak, just looking at her. She tried to remember looking like that, ever. *She's a schoolteacher*, she thought in disbelief.

She imagined Ichabod Crane in a one-room schoolhouse. She thought of *Little House on the Prairie*. She didn't once think of a woman like Emily Mueller.

Emily came out, smiling and waving at her dowdy old friend, and trailing just a couple feet behind her was a man. Tall, with a bit of a belly, but not too much, a hairy chest that bristled out of the top buttons of his shirt. He had a short beard and a balding head and big, comical glasses that made him look like he was wearing a Halloween costume. He looked up with a shy smile and waved too, sheepishly.

"Hope you don't mind," she said, heading her off. "But I brought Wilbur. Don't worry, he doesn't bite."

Carina smiled thinly, while trying to seem warm. "It's nice to meet you finally, Wilbur. I've heard so much about you."

In their monthly phone calls, when Steve was safely out of the house, Emily talked non-stop about her husband. For nearly seventeen years, she'd heard about Wilbur, but until then had never met him.

"You as well," he said. "Carina, that's a pretty name. Is that Italian?"

"My father was Italian," she said. "But my mother was from the Philippines."

He nodded, as if to make a mental note of her complexion. "Well, it's nice to finally meet you."

During their dinner together, Carina felt on edge, but every time she was sure of an imminent outburst, none occurred. Emily ordered the wrong drink for Wilbur and Carina silently braced, knowing fully well she was about to witness a familiar domestic drama.

But Wilbur shrugged. "It's fine, I'll go figure it out."

They looked at her when she sighed in relief.

She was waiting for blood to boil, anger to show its ugly face—transforming his normal, banal countenance into something commonly demonic.

But he said nothing. His eyebrows didn't flare, his teeth never showed. He simply adjusted his corduroy blazer and looked bashful. Carina didn't know what to do, so she said, "Excuse me, sorry. Real quick."

She was glad that Emily didn't follow her to the restroom, saying that she too had to go, where she would have to hear her the stall over, gushing about her perfect, quiet life in rural Oregon. When Carina made it into the bathroom, she removed her mask and began to sob.

Hot tears rolled down her cheeks. She stared at herself in the mirror and asked herself questions, some of them silent, some of them aloud.

"How did I get like this?" she wondered.

"What has he done to me?"

"Who am I?"

Carina washed her face in the sink, her lower lip quivering. At one point, she realized her life had been straightforward. She had settled into her lifestyle, languidly deforming like a glass window given time.

But now, with fire—she was warped and melting, bending light into curves. The lens through which she saw her life had been revealed to her by one simple interaction: a husband, kind and meek and difficult to provoke.

When she went back to the table, she was flushed.

"Are you alright, Cari?"

"Yeah, fine."

Wilbur looked at her, marvelously obtuse. "Is there something wrong? Can I get you something?"

"No, absolutely not," she said. "I just realized something. I don't need any help right now. I'm fine." She took a deep breath. Suddenly, she was dazzled by her future. The potential of it. The music of it. Everything it could be. Before, she saw it as a song she'd heard a thousand times before. "Resentful Couple Cohabitates Until They Rot in D Minor." She knew the melody, knew how it resolved. She'd seen it sung a million times before. But now . . . now, she was singing a new song. One she didn't know she had the pipes for.

"How is teaching?" she asked, eager for time, time she only had away from Steve Calico.

Emily told her all about it, willingly, happily. She told her about her smart students, who amazed her every day with what they'd learned. She told her about the homey feeling of the town, the administrators who were actually worth a damn. She told her about the charm of the place. "God damn, you wouldn't believe this place. They still have an honest to goodness video store."

Carina nodded along to it all and she thought about Steve, who so often called her stupid. There was Wilbur across from her, and she couldn't imagine him ever saying anything like that. She tried to imagine them fighting, but she assumed, like with most things, Emily had built their relationship in such a way that even their arguments were quiet disagreements, instigated without heat or anger or jealous rage. She knew, for a fact, that they told each other "I love you" often and sweetly, but not laboriously. It came off their lips as natural as air.

Carina listened to everything she had to say, and kept them talking much longer than any of them had planned.

"Sounds wonderful," she said dreamily.

But really, she was writing a song.

<hr>

When she got back from shopping, she checked every corner of her apartment the way she always did. She had no reason to be so cautious, she knew, but it was not something she could help.

She opened each closet quickly, she threw open every door.

There was nobody home, of course. There never was.

He didn't even know where she lived now. She'd made sure of that.

She didn't want him to be angry with her.

She hoped he was happier, that his rage had dissipated and that he could just leave her alone, for good.

Somehow though, Carina felt that was too good to be true.

She walked to the stove and cooked up a meager meal of cup noodles. There was nothing else for her here, she decided. Nothing at all. And when the noodles were gone, she looked out across her apartment and noted the boxes—the many, many boxes—and knew it would only be days before she was gone.

Her phone rang.

She pulled it out, carefully, avoiding its flat black screen for a moment, hoping it wasn't anything old and familiar catching up with her.

Good, she thought.

She lifted the phone to her ear.

"Hey, girl," said Emily, her voice infectious. "Are you ready for the big move?"

"I am," said Carina sullenly. "I think it's all sorted."

"And what about Steve?"

What about Steve?

"He's not my problem anymore," she said.

Emily lowered her tone, almost to a whisper. "You're doing the right thing."

"I know, I know."

There was silence, a short pause, before Emily's voice brightened again. "But," she said, "this is exciting. This will be good for you. This is an adventure."

"Yes," Carina agreed, staring out the window at a new car she didn't recognize parking in a neighbor's parking spot, when usually said neighbor was at work. "I just hope I'm not imposing," she said, absently.

"Nonsense, nonsense. You're going to be our guinea pig."

"Oh yeah?"

She held her breath as the car door opened, nearly dinging the vehicle beside it.

"It's a fact. We figured you'd need your own space, at least for a little while."

"I'm probably not gonna stay forever."

The man got out. Tall, white, leather jacket—

Blond hair.

A stranger.

Good.

"Of course not. You need to find where you want to be, hon. We know that. But we're happy to have you until everything blows over, or whatever. Wilbur just got a big bonus from his firm and we're thinking of starting a B & B as a little side hustle. You know how it is."

Carina shook her head. She didn't. Carina could barely afford her own apartment, let alone two houses.

"It's this little farmhouse, right on the outskirts of town," she continued, "and I think you're going to love it. It's cozy, spacious, and we're going to have the full thing furnished before you arrive. So, it's going to be nice."

"You guys didn't have to go through the trouble."

"It's no trouble at all," said Emily, reminding Carina, once again, that her and Wilbur were better off than she could ever dream.

"Thank you," she said.

For the rest of the phone call, they went over the details of the move as if they were planning a heist. They were playing spy, an act that Carina found some joy in, because it made her feel as if she were in control.

"You'll fly into Portland."

"And you'll be waiting at six?"

"On the dot."

"Then: a two hour drive."

"Right, to the heartland."

When the call ended, they both had the satisfaction of a good game played. Before she hung up, Carina thanked her one more time. Then, alone, she closed her blinds—for the sake of her sanity.

Chapter Four

Wʜᴇʀᴇ ᴛʜᴇ ꜰᴜᴄᴋ *is everyone?*

Steve Calico grabbed the collar of his brown leather jacket and held it close to his neck. Fucking cold, he thought, but it was only September, and not very deep into it. But it was also midnight, and sometimes nights were just that cold.

He walked down the empty street and looked at empty storefronts, boarded up with plywood with signs that claimed: Store is empty, nothing to steal.

Nice part of town.

There was a slight breeze, and even in the city, it brought with it the scent of Autumnal elegance. Leaves, captured in their slow, dry deaths—like an herbal tea made with dust and honey.

This was where he'd grown up. This was where a part of him would always remain.

Steve looked up and down the street, looking for any sign of life, but there was none. He thought about yelling. Maybe if he yelled loud enough he'd see—

There.

A kid.

On the corner.

There was always a kid on the corner.

Seventeen, maybe. Black. Dressed in Carhartts and a Ravens hat, he was looking down at his phone as his breath clouded in front of his face. Steve walked toward him. "Hey, man," he said, trying not to startle him.

The kid jerked his head in a greeting. "You looking for something?"

"Crank," he said.

"I don't got no crank."

"What?"

"No crank."

"What do you got then?"

"Girls."

The kid's eyes went back down to his phone, as if he were merely looking up directions.

"You ain't heard that from me though."

Steve smiled. "Well, well, well. How does the song go? You can't always get—"

The kid cut him off. "I don't know that fucking song, man. You want pussy or not?"

Steve thought about how easy it would be to drag the kid into an alley and beat him. It was a lonely street. No one would give a flying fuck about what happened to a poor Black kid selling his girlfriend's ass, but Steve stood still, eyeing him up and down. He didn't know what was under the kid's jacket. One wrong move and he'd have his brains blown out all over an open sewer.

"Maybe I can see her."

The kid pointed down the street. "You can see her from here."

Sure enough, Steve followed his finger and saw the woman in question. More of a child, really. She couldn't have been any older than the kid.

Steve's lips twisted into one of his wolfish smiles. "Wow, that's some fine wares you got there, son."

"I'm not your fuckin' son, man."

"Say, now tell me this straight—is that your girlfriend?"

The boy looked at him in disgust, his nose wriggling up, his lips parting as if a rotten taste had crept into his mouth. "Who do you think you are, man? Stop playing games or we'll end it right now. My girlfriend . . . motherfucker." Steve was hoping to see something in the kid's reaction, some inner truth. He wanted him to say that she was, because, somehow, that excited him deeply. He very much wanted her to be young and taken, because it wasn't enough to fuck her. He wanted to feel like he'd taken her.

"Alright, fine. Who do I pay?"

"Me, now."

They made their negotiations in hushed whispers and soon Steve was dropping several large bills in the kid's hands.

It'd been a while since he'd been with a woman. God knew his wife—ex-wife—wasn't one to show anyone a good time. While her libido dive-bombed over the years, his became all the more explosive, all the more intolerably burdensome.

He hadn't planned on this at all, but sometimes—sometimes—you got what you needed.

He walked down the street casually, not like a nervous john, but like a professional himself. A man about town who knew about such worldly things, a man who had and will do this a thousand times before and a thousand times again.

The girl didn't look at him. Instead, she looked down at her feet, then away, and then, finally, when he was just within a couple feet of her, she took a glance at him up and down. "Where are we going?" she asked.

He motioned to his car. "Somewhere safe."

"It's safe here," she said.

"Somewhere private."

She didn't argue. He could hear the tremor in her voice. *God*, he thought, *she is young. Real young.* Steve Calico led her by the arm, he used a soft touch, a gentleman's touch, and even opened his car door for her. He waved to the kid down the street, who was still standing on the corner, and was now smoking a cigarette he couldn't buy himself. He didn't wave back.

"You gotta bring me back here," she said.

"Sure, sure. We're not going too far. Just a hotel. Too cold to do anything in the car."

"Okay," she said, sounding more comfortable, if only by a degree.

They didn't talk. Steve drove silently down empty streets in the unseasonable cold. He didn't know where he was taking her. He just wanted to take her. Sometimes, when he was nearing a hotel, he could hear her breath soften, her spirit become hopeful—and as soon as this hopefulness appeared, he'd change directions and she'd grip the door handle.

Finally, she said. "I don't got all night."

"I know," said Steve.

"We gotta pick a place soon." Her voice cracked, a fact of which she seemed embarrassed.

"I don't have all night either. Soon."

At a stoplight, he looked at the girl. She probably didn't go to school anymore. Where were her parents in all of this?

He asked, "Was that guy at the corner, was he your boyfriend?"

"Mike? No, Mike's my brother."

"Good brother," he said.

"We look out for each other."

"I'm sure you do."

Steve gripped the wheel. "Put your head down."

"I'm not doing it while you're—"

"Just do it!"

Red and blue lights flashed behind him as she ducked her head down. Steve watched them barrel toward him, a kaleidoscope of terror in his rearview mirror.

Keep it together.

Nothing wrong here, officer. Just giving the girl a ride home. She's my—

"If he asks, you're my niece," he said. "Got that?'

"Yes," she murmured, her head still down.

The lights got closer, a constellation. Sirens blared like the call of the wild hunt and Steve Calico felt hunted. "Jesus Christ."

The cruiser passed him in a blur.

"Thank God."

The girl poked her head up. "Is it over?"

Steve watched the cop car disappear into the distance at lightning speed. "I think so," he said.

He pulled over, his hands sweating on the wheel of the car. "Go ahead, get out."

"C'mon, man. You gotta take me home."

"I don't have to do shit. Get out."

The girl opened the door and stepped out onto the sidewalk, she held her arms close to her body. She was shivering and Steve watched the cold creep through her baby fat as her eyes went wet. Now that he'd seen her like this—suffering—he almost wanted her again.

The distant wail of a siren made him tense up.

"Plenty more pussy out there," he mumbled to himself. "Plenty more." He turned away from the girl.

"Wait!" she called.

And again he wanted to watch her shiver, to watch her beg for him.

But he was already gone.

As he drove away, he was angry. His knuckles were white on the wheel. *Whole lotta trouble for nothing.*

Rage boiled, though. The worst kind of rage—the kind where a guy only had himself to blame.

But then he had an idea.

Maybe tonight can be saved after all, he thought. *Wait til the boys hear about this.*

He had let Carina have her time away from him, he had let her play her game—she was playing the role of the battered spouse—a role he found pathetic. But still, she had done her part, and now it was time to do his.

Steve stepped on the gas.

Carina was never as careful as she thought she was. He laughed about it, barreling down the empty streets with nothing but a hard-on and ideas. He'd show that bitch, he'd show her good—and then what would happen? She'd squeal? Maybe . . . unless.

He imagined how her head would feel between his palms.

He often went back to the night when she told him he was leaving, where after nearly two decades of weak slaps and shoves he finally made good on what his body told him he wanted. He felt her cartilage break against his knuckles. She cried. She bled. He kept going, working on her as a painter would on a sufficiently laborious painting. He liked the way she looked when he hit her, and he knew neither of them would ever be able to forget that night.

Hitting was only one thing a man could do.

He could end it all if he wanted to.

Steve whistled. He knew the old girl's address. He wasn't stupid. It only took a couple calls to shared accounts, some of those easy chuckles and friendly questions. *Oh God, this is a total dumbo move—but my wife and I just moved—and I can't seem to remember . . . Oh jeez, do you mind confirming our current address for me?* It was easy. But he'd been cautious. He'd stayed back.

He'd watched her come and go.

From afar, Steve Calico watched as her face healed, as she tried to change who she was. But he didn't touch, no, because he knew there'd be a day when he needed to touch her. The day when he'd finally end her. He clicked his teeth. The fantasy was seductive.

He pulled into his ex-wife's parking lot, turned off the ignition, and sat.

Do you really wanna do this, man? Do you really wanna be the crazy ex? You're not a killer, man.

No, of course not.

But do I want to be?

He considered the thought for a moment before getting out of the car. A great gravity came over him, as if he had just taken on a mythic task. He was Odysseus, Hercules, Ulysses. He was the judge and the jury, and yes, sometimes, when he wasn't so afraid, the executioner too.

He walked calmly through the parking lot.

I can turn back now.

I should turn back now.

He idled by the bushes. He felt sober and worse because of it. His erection had disappeared and he was left creeping around shrubbery like a run-of-the-mill prowler.

This isn't me, he thought. *I don't have to be like this.*

But he was really too close to turn around. He didn't have a choice. He wished he did, but today, all he could do was follow his impulse, that great and demanding muse that had led his life thus far.

She had a ground-floor apartment, he knew.

He knew just where, too. He followed the windows until he found the one, and when he found it, he approached it with great reverence. There was no one out at this time, no one to see him. And if he only got a glimpse of her, of her home, he could feel like he won. *You got her under your thumb, my man. Nothing to worry about. Scope her out, go home, get drunk, jerk off.*

Dumb bitch left the windows open.

She'd gone through the trouble of covering her tracks, of disappearing, but couldn't even be bothered to close her blinds.

He peered inside to the absolute blackness.

His eyes adjusted slowly and soon he was scrambling for his phone, grinding his teeth.   *What the fuck?*

Flashlight.

White light shined from the camera flash and he could see it all clearly.

His rage spiked; jaw muscles clenched. For a moment, he considered screaming, loud and long into the night.

The apartment was empty.

It was all gone.

Carina had up and left, and Steve Calico was alone.

Chapter Five

SHE WATCHED EACH passenger carefully as they came aboard.

He's much too gangly.

No purpose to his movements.

Too genuine.

Too sad.

Not sad enough.

There were a million characteristics that she could come up with to make a man not Steve Calico.

She felt safest thousands of feet in the air. The clouds were like some beautiful impressionist painting, the kind that when she was a kid, would've stolen her breath away in a single glance. She read, thought, and occasionally doodled on a pad of paper she'd brought, optimistically, as if there was a chance for her to rediscover that buried part of her that used to do such things, who used to have interests. That was what no one told you about being under someone's thumb—that as time went on, you lost all semblance of yourself.

Carina tried to find these pieces of herself along the way to Greentree, hoping to arrive intact. She daydreamed of being someone to wow Emily. Someone successful, healthy—a magnet that could light up a room. But the thought made her wilt. It was not easy to be someone else—even in her head. She swallowed, tried to conjure the self-care, the positive self-talk that Emily spoke about in uninterrupted streams of syllables. *There was time now— time to change, metamorphosize, become new. Or whatever.*

The plane arrived in Portland and she felt her breath leave her body.

The sky was slate gray and endless, tickled by the tops of tall pines and firs. As the plane reached its terminal, she craned her neck to see her surroundings. She'd never been to the west coast before, she'd never thought she'd ever make it out this far.

Everything was either concrete or trees—which made for a soothing, if not cold color palette of greens and grays. *There's a city here, somewhere,* she thought.

As promised, Emily was there waiting. She looked the same as ever. Beautiful, stunning, with big eyes and a trim figure. Her blonde hair was cut shorter than before, hanging just at her neckline. She wore black leggings and a turtleneck. *Chic,* thought Carina. *That's the word for it. She looks chic.*

When she saw Carina, she leapt up and down, waving. "Get over here!" she squealed and Carina couldn't help but catch her enthusiasm. She ran to her old friend, her carry-on bag rocking behind her on unsteady wheels.

They hugged, they smiled, and Emily asked, over and over: "You're okay, right? You said you're okay?"

"I'm fine, so far so good."

"He hasn't tried anything, has he?"

"Not that I know of, no."

"Good, that's good."

Emily led her to the car, chattering nonstop about the drive, where they would be going, what to expect.

"Now, I'm going to warn you. Greentree is small. Like, real small. But it has its charms, for sure. I know it'll take some getting used to, but believe me, we're here for you. Anything you need, Wilbur and I have your back." Then, after a long pause came what Emily really wanted to say, almost as an afterthought, under her breath as she turned the ignition. "I never liked Steve, anyways."

Carina, who usually kept her true self hidden, let drop her facade. "I never liked him either." Her voice quaked and Emily reached out to pat her shoulder.

"I know, hon, I know. We do what we think is best and when it doesn't work out, we keep moving. Like a shark." She made a playful biting sound, to release the tension and Carina smiled.

"I've been scared," she admitted.

"Well, you picked a good place then."

"Why?"

"Because, in Greentree, Steve would be spotted in a half-minute if he came to town. Greentree's just like that. You're an outsider too, they'll be all up in your grill. That's just the way it is. But don't worry, they'll get used to you."

"How long have you been there now?"

"Just a year. But it's been a good year."

Carina nodded. Since college, Emily had been tenacious with keeping in contact. She'd carefully documented every life event, every move with a long email. Carina wasn't sure why Emily was her friend, because in comparison, her own life was so dull, so unfortunate. In her darkest moments, she considered Emily's friendship as charity. Other times, she thought she must be supremely lonely. Lonelier than even herself.

"I'm sure I'll love it," said Carina.

"Well, I hope so. I really do."

She left it at that for the time being and they enjoyed the landscapes. It began to drizzle and Carina felt some inner stirring, that she was indeed in a new place starting a new life and the old one was so far away it might as well be unimaginable. This new place was teeming with life.

But the further Emily took the car, the more life changed. They'd been on the road an hour and the suburban sprawl had dissipated into small townships and farms. Hop farms stretched across the horizon—automatic sprinklers lining their rows with brushed metal.

And in another half hour, Emily looked at her and smiled, as if she knew. "We're getting close," she said. "Don't worry. It's not too much further."

And now, it was all farmland, rolling hills that were vast and eternal. Civilization out here was limited to scattered large towns. There were wineries and breweries advertised on billboards, but Carina could never tell where those places might be. When she looked at the exits, they all seemed to lead to more fields.

"Over there," said Emily, motioning so far down the road that Carina couldn't quite tell where she was motioning. "That's where we're going."

She squinted her eyes and saw black shapes. *The trees are back*, she thought with some elation. She did not know why she was excited, only that those tall pines had become comforting. The trees that seemed to touch the low ceiling of the sky were a symbol.

Without the trees, they could be anywhere. Because of those tall icons of wood and needles, they were here.

Greentree announced itself with a quaint sign that said nothing more than "Welcome to Greentree! Population 2,860." There were trees, yes, but the rest of the town was flat and brown. It was charming, for certain, but it was not what Carina had imagined. With a name like Greentree, she expected it to be some lush, hidden community with houses built on tree branches twenty feet off the earth. But that wasn't likely or possible, she had to remind herself.

Seeing it now, she tried to separate it from fantasy.

Greentree was small, but there were people on the street. Emily guided them through it with sure hands, passing down Main Street where Carina eyed the downtown as if she would be asked to draw it from memory later. *There were so many shops*, she thought. The town was positively bustling. Then, downtown was behind them and just like Emily said, there was a little video store, the Stardust, sitting in a prime location on its main drag. *The town was normal*, she thought. But also, more than that. *Vital.*

"Most of them are small business owners, some farmers," said Emily suddenly, as if apologizing. "It's not the big city, but they're good folk."

"I like it. It's nice. It looks quiet."

Emily laughed. "It's certainly quiet. Very quiet."

Past the long fields of wheat, there were the trees again. They were like the outer walls of a castle, keeping Greentree protected, safe from the outside world. The sky was still gray and the rain still fell, but Greentree was tucked away where nothing but rain could find it.

Emily's car slowed to a crawl as she drove further still, taking the turns of an old country road with the deftest touch. "We're on the outskirts here, but not much longer. Just up ahead."

A little longer, and: "There, right there."

Emily was talking about the white house, up on a small hill, where other white houses stood, but distanced away from each other, as if each had mutually agreed that they all needed their own space. It was a two-story house with a big yard, front and back, and a spacious porch. Steve would've called it a sitcom house.

Carina resisted the urge to comment on how large it was. Back when she was with Steve, they lived in a number of apartments, always moving when rent got hiked. Steve was always looking over his shoulder, wondering about the neighbors and everyone else. He'd talk about houses as if they were as inevitable as death, as if one day the biological metanarrative would force him into one whether he liked it or not. But, at least as long as Carina was there, no such inevitability happened. Their final fight was in a two-bedroom apartment, right before Steve had to go to work.

It was the only way she could be sure he would leave. Steve was never late.

"Alright, here we are. Home sweet home."

Wilbur stepped out onto the porch. In the time since she'd seen him, he'd grown a ponytail, despite his balding head. He smiled with big, crooked teeth and waved them both in. He looked like a stoner-savant math professor; a Carl Sagan devotee who decorated with beaded curtains and psychedelic art.

"Welcome, welcome," he said. He pulled Emily close to him and then planted a ferocious kiss on her lips. Carina averted her gaze, uncomfortable at their public affection.

"Well, you made it," said Wilbur. "How was the trip?"

"Good, pretty. I didn't realize how many trees there were out here." She felt stupid saying it aloud, but had nothing else to say.

Wilbur shrugged, oblivious to her nervousness. "Yeah, trees and breweries. That's what we got up here. It's a pretty place," he said, eyes focusing in on the middle-distance. Then, "Let's get you inside. You'll want to settle down. Em told you about the farmhouse, right? Our future endeavor?"

Carina nodded. "Yes, it sounds lovely. But, you really didn't have to go through so much trouble."

"It's no trouble," he said. "None at all. Just know that it won't be ready until tomorrow. That's when our local government will finally take their time turning the power on, the bastards."

He didn't say it seriously, Carina noted. He wasn't really mad.

Emily touched her arm and led her forward. Their home was immaculate, beautiful, it looked new, like it hadn't been lived in yet.

"Where's Hazel?" asked Emily to Wilbur.

Wilbur shrugged. "Doing her Goth shit, I suppose."

Emily slapped her husband's arm playfully. She wasn't mad

either. "Our daughter is going through her edgy phase. Very Alanis Morrisette."

Wilbur shook his head in mock exasperation. "*Mom, that is so not goth.*"

"Yeah, welcome to our life."

Carina followed them through their home, saying nice things and listening to the world in the background, to the noises Greentree made. It chirped with birds, whistled with soft winds. She could smell hay and manure and decaying leaves. Through her host's windows, she could see glimpses of the blood red sunset. *I think I could stay here forever*, she thought. *If it'll have me.*

CHAPTER SIX

SHE WOKE UP SWEATING. Silver light lined her room.

Oh God oh God oh God he's here. Get me out of here, get me out!

She took fistfuls of her blankets in her hands. Her eyes weren't adjusting. *See, goddamnit! I can't see! I can't see anything! He's come for me and I can't see!*

Slowly, the contours of her bedroom came into focus. She jerked her head left, right, up and down, then ducked down off the bed, to look under the frame—

Nothing.

She sat on her bed. The black of her doorway was clearing like mist. She blinked. She blinked again and the doorway was clearer still. She strained her eyes, because *something* was there, *something* was—

And then she saw it.

In the door.

She exhaled.

A girl.

She suddenly became aware that she was sweating. She was soaked. She brushed her bangs off of her forehead and tried to calm her breathing.

"Hello, Hazel," she said.

The girl in the doorway, with black dyed hair and raccoon eye makeup was about sixteen years old. She stood there, stone silent.

"Is there something I can help you with?"

Hazel didn't answer.

Maybe she was sleepwalking, she thought.

"Hazel?"

Carina's eyes adjusted. No wonder she couldn't see her at first, the girl was dressed in black from head to toe.

Hazel stood in the doorway, bored yet defiant. A middle-finger casually outstretched.

"It was just a nightmare," said Carina, more to herself. She sounded like she'd just run a marathon.

The girl in the doorway shook her head. "Fucking freak."

By the time Carina thought of something to say, the girl in the doorway had drifted away, and Carina had drifted to sleep.

"We'll have to show you around, properly," said Emily.

"Yes, it would be a shame not to show you what ol' Greentree has to offer, I mean, if you're going to be here for a while."

Carina thought she heard resentment in Wilbur's voice, however masked. But she'd learned long ago that her perception was not to be trusted. She heard slights everywhere, they followed her in every sentence spoken, with little knives at the ready.

"Not that that's a problem," he said quickly.

Emily's lips pursed. "It's not a problem at all. When I saw what he did to you . . . I just couldn't."

Carina's insides scrunched up. It was as if she wasn't even there.

Wilbur nodded. "No, of course. A man like that should be locked up."

But instead of saying anything, she swallowed it down. Tried to change the subject; talk about the coffee, the eggs, the department store decor, anything.

They were sitting at the breakfast table, the three of them. Hazel had already slinked wordlessly out the door to school, nervously twisting the jelly bracelets on her wrist, earbuds buried deep into her skull. She didn't look at Carina but Carina couldn't take her eyes off of her.

Here was a strange creature—a forgotten echo of every girl who became a woman—the teenage daughter. Carina found herself thoughtfully considering every aspect of Hazel. She admired her territorial fierceness. Carina wished to bottle it, drink it, and make it her own.

"How does Hazel feel about Greentree?" she asked.

Emily shrugged and Carina suddenly felt herself slipping into Hazel's Doc Martens.

"She's a teenager," said Emily, as if that explained everything. "You can never tell with them."

Wilbur smiled. "I used to be a rocker when I was her age. Maybe that's what it is. She won't tell us shit though. But who would?"

"I was an angry teenager too," said Carina.

Emily looked at her, with eyes narrowed to slits. "The way you talk, I always thought you came into being as a mature twenty-two year old."

"I was that, twenty years ago," Carina said.

Emily's mouth opened wide, delighted. "What a spark plug!"

"It was my parents that were the problem, at least they were for me, at that age. They weren't from here and I couldn't stand how they couldn't get a grip on English. I mean, they spoke English, but not like I spoke it. They always sounded like foreigners, with an accent, and I'd get so embarrassed." Carina looked down at her plate. "I'd beg them not to come to the plays I was in. I just couldn't handle the idea of someone hearing my parents talk."

"We only know what it's like to grow up while we're doing it," said Wilbur.

"Ain't that the truth."

"Now, that they're dead . . . I don't know if I would've done anything different," said Carina. "They were the ones who pushed me to marry Steve right out of college. They didn't think I'd be able to find work in the Arts." Carina stared at her friend, a sad smile creeping over her lips. Her parents' deaths were a piece of the puzzle—a last act of love. Without a small inheritance, she would've had to stay. Without Emily, she wouldn't have known what to do. "I wanted to thank you again for having me."

"Oh, you don't have to—"

"I know, but I want to let you know, this means a lot to me. I feel like I've lived under other people's thumbs my entire life and I want this to be the first time I'm not. I woke up last night—" she paused, "and I realized I didn't know who I was."

"You're my friend," said Emily.

"You're you," offered Wilbur.

"I'm a mold that other people pour themselves into," she said with a laugh. "And I've been so pleasantly uncomplicated for so long, that I've allowed it to happen and happen again. And I'm tired of it."

Emily took her hand. "You look so alive, already."

"I am," said Carina, remembering something she loved so long ago. "I am I am I am."

After breakfast, Emily took her to see the town. "I have some errands, but I thought you could keep me company, if you like."

"I wanted to pick up some art supplies anyways," said Carina. She almost felt normal, like Greentree was already rubbing off on her. It was easy here. It was easy not to listen for footsteps or watch for dark-haired men.

Emily drove, running her errands, while Carina wondered more about their conversation that morning. She analyzed her reactions, her own needs. She navel-gazed to her heart's content, trying to find the secret to whatever made her who she was. She had been a housewife for so many years, she was Steve's ball and chain, she was a sponge for hate, she was a decorative ornament. But now, old feelings came up and she was no longer concerned with survival, so she sat with these feelings and tried to make sense of them.

Carina coped—but she did not let go, not ever. She remembered the violent night that changed her life, the crescendo to decades of lesser violence, that turned her from frightened dependent to frightened independent. She remembered and relived the terror she felt when she had her first panic attack, when she was a spectacle. And now, she felt that she was a guest, a burden, a charity case. While Emily ran her errands, she tried to make those feelings pass too.

"There's a craft store here, surprisingly," she said, getting back into the car. "We've got a lot more than you'd think."

It was only a five minute drive, because really, everything was only a five minute drive. They parked in the ample parking lot of the video store. Carina looked at her questioningly.

"It's around back," she explained. "But Larry's got the room, so everyone parks here."

"Who?"

"Larry Dell. He's the owner of the Stardust." She said it as if everyone knew Larry Dell, as if he were a Greentree pillar. "I need to return some DVDs anyways. But take your time."

Carina felt like she was in another world. *I need to return some DVDs.*

She walked past the Stardust, rubber-necking the whole way. It was somehow too quaint for even Greentree. It was something out of time. She cursed the fact that she was now old enough to consider video rentals a fair addition to Norman Rockwell's americana.

The craft store was more what she expected. Paints and yarn were timeless. They were of the physical realm. It was a small store with low ceilings that was longer than it was wide. In fact, the whole store had a narrowness in its quality that made Carina feel like she was traveling down the length of a needle. Still, she found her supplies quickly—a four pack of small canvases, each a little larger than standard printer paper, acrylic brushes, and a bevy of paint tubes.

The woman at the counter, an older woman with thick glasses and gray hair looked at each item as if they were a window into Carina's soul. "Well, now," she said softly. "It seems you'll be doing some painting."

"Yes, I think so."

She looked up at her. "Are you a painter?"

"A long time ago, I dabbled. I'm thinking of taking it up again."

"Well. That's nice." She narrowed her vision. "I haven't seen you before."

"No, I'm new," said Carina.

"Oh my, a rare treat. We don't see many new folks around here."

"I'm staying with some friends."

"Do these friends have names?"

"Emily and Wilbur Mueller."

The woman seemed to smirk. "Ah, those two."

"Yes?"

"Oh, nothing. I'm sure they're fine people. I don't know them so well myself."

Carina looked at the old woman, who seemed to be relishing her own tight lips. Finally, Carina said, "But?"

"Well, they're rather new themselves. Not exactly lifers."

"Oh, no. Yes, I guess that's true. They moved from the city."

The woman nodded slowly. "Yes, not that there's anything

wrong with it, mind you. We need new blood in this little town every once in a while." She smiled, bagging the paints. "Now, there you go, dear. Bring one of your paintings by sometime. I'd love to see your work."

Carina left the shop backwards, waving and smiling and wondering if there was anything there for her to hold onto, to relive and remember forever.

She hoped there wasn't.

Outside, she turned around and around, as if she were lost. *What should I be doing right now?*

Assert myself. Take control. Be unafraid.

She walked to the video store, just steps away, then paused in the parking lot.

Steve never liked to watch movies. He'd get antsy during them. He'd stand up and walk around or find something to do, anything but sit and watch. "Why do you watch that shit?" he'd ask. "None of it's real."

Carina would just sit quietly. She'd say, "I'm not hurting you by watching a movie."

He'd wave her off, sometimes leave. Carina liked movies.

Through the windows of the Stardust, she saw Emily, deep in smiling conversation. Carina pushed through the doors. The smell of popcorn coated her lungs in buttery slickness. She stood in the lobby for a moment, experiencing the past. Emily was talking to a man with short gray hair and a teal polo and at first she wasn't sure if she should interrupt, if maybe it'd be better to stand back and wait, but it wasn't long until Emily signaled her entrance.

"Larry, here's my friend." She motioned Carina forward.

"This is Carina," she said. "She's staying with us for a bit, trying on Greentree to see how it fits."

Larry shook her hand. "Well, well, well—we don't get many newcomers here."

Carina smiled. "So, I've heard. The woman next door said the same thing."

"Well, that old bat is bound to say anything. I should know, she's my mother."

Emily nodded. "Two generations of family business here." She said it as if it were a line, and after she said it, Carina caught her side-eyeing Larry for approval.

"Greentree has been kind to us, indeed," said Larry.

Carina looked around the store. "This is a nice place you got here."

The movies were divided by genre, lovingly alphabetized. The new releases wrapped around the wall and then stopped and continued, before and after, an awning. The opening there was covered in a beaded curtain. Above it, a placard read: Adults Only.

"You have to be over eighteen to go in there," said Larry with a smile, following her gaze.

Emily laughed. "Go ahead, show him your I.D."

They chatted a while, light and easy. Larry was an excellent conversationalist and whenever he or Emily would begin talking about Greentree or the school or anything else Carina knew nothing about, he'd apologize and shoot a question her way.

"Let me guess—you're from out east?"

"How did you know? I don't have an accent."

Larry shrugged, almost bashful. "Lucky guess. Are you going to stay?"

"I hadn't thought about it," she responded honestly. "I don't know."

"Well, consider it," he said. "Work is good for the bones and everything around them. I could always take you on here, you know."

"I'll keep that in mind," she said.

When Emily was done catching up, mostly on local gossip and how the newest cashiers were doing at the Stardust, they left. In the car, Carina couldn't help but ask, "How does a video store stay in business here? I mean, doesn't everyone use Netflix now?"

"I'm sure they do. We do, occasionally. But there's a lot of enthusiasm for local businesses here. 'Buy Greentree' and all of that."

"And it works, doesn't it?"

Emily shrugged. "It seems like everything here has existed forever. Larry Dell's sort of a legend around here, the local businessman that did good. He hires the teenagers. He's probably been half the town's boss at one point or another."

"He could be mine, too."

Emily gave her a side-eye. "You don't have to work. You need to heal."

"I can do both at the same time. I mean, you heard it: work is good for the bones and everything around them."

"That's Larry-speak. He says that kind of shit all the time. Just please, promise me one thing."

"What's that?"

"Focus on healing. Nothing else. Let everything else go."

"For a while," she said, needling her friend. "Then, I'm going to bury my pain and work, work, work until my bones become strong."

"Oh, God," Emily groaned. "Alright, enough errands. Let's check out the B & B."

They went down a curving road, past pastures and shrubbery, and it was the closest Carina had been to the wall of trees that grew around the village. They were tall and ominous, but also coddling, protective.

The house was on the horizon. Two stories. Warm and softly pink, like a cocktail of blood and milk. Around it: acres and acres of dying corn stalks.

"I think you're going to love it here," said Emily. "I think it's really a nice place."

The house was something out of a movie, and she immediately thought of Larry Dell—which made her twitch, because she had only known of Larry Dell for ten minutes and now somehow, he was inextricably linked to everything Greentree was.

But it was beautiful. And evocative.

She imagined the house as it would look in different seasons, starting at the beginning of the year, where it would be encrusted with snow in the center of a flat field of dead crops.

Then, the spring—where the house was now bright and airy and the soil around it was rich and dark and freshly tilled. Carina closed her eyes. She saw the sun high in the air with crisp, blue skies. Flowers blossomed and a black bearded farmer with overalls was sipping ale in the evening, admiring his works. His wife sat beside him and held his hands. His children ran out far into the field and he didn't call for them because he could see for miles, right up to the giant, tall—

"Here we are."

Summer now. Sweltering hot. The sun is a torch. The farmer is riding a tractor, the corn has grown very tall. The children dart in and out of the rows, disappearing within them like it's some secret world, one that only they could ever know. The farmer mops his brow and smokes a corn cob pipe, his wife has all the doors and window open and she's making dinner. The trees don't seem so close now, so threatening, the sun keeps them away. Everyone is happy and safe and—

When Carina opened her eyes, the car had stopped.

"What do you think?"

She was seeing the house for the first time, right in front of her. And she was seeing it in autumn. The air was mild and the endless corn had begun to turn. The chill in the air was already working on the green, edging them with chestnut streaks of decay. She got out of the car. The ranch house looked lonely. She didn't have the nerve to tell Emily this, that it felt like a lonely place. She surveyed the land, her hand forming a visor over her eyes.

"Looks beautiful," she said. "Cozy."

Where the corn fields ended, sat those impressive, gargantuan pines—a wall of them. Carina was used to feeling small, used to cowering before those bigger and stronger, but she was not used to feeling this minuscule, this invisible. She felt like an ant when compared to those impressive giants—they were older and had weathered more than she could ever imagine.

"Let's poke around for a minute, make sure everything works." After she said it, she grabbed Carina's arm. "Everything's okay, isn't it? You're alright?"

Carina took her friend's hands in her own. She almost shuddered. It'd been too long since she'd felt warm skin on hers.. "I'm good," she said.

"Because, if this is too much for you, if you'd rather be around people, we can—"

"No, I want to get to know myself. I need to spend some time alone, away from others."

Emily nodded and took her by the arm. The sun was beginning to set, red and orange on the horizon, fighting heavy rain clouds for dominion of the cosmos. "In that case, let's get you settled."

Carina sat on the front porch of the house, alone.

It was indeed beautiful. The furniture was brand new, the room prepared for her was spacious and welcoming. The decor was rustic but never cloying. The kitchen was stocked with cast iron pans that looked decades old. She felt like she had vanished—gone from the modern world—to a place where no one could ever find her. This pleased her deeply, to vanish.

The house was perfect, in that way.

Sitting on that front porch with her tea and the blood-red sun setting like an impressionist painting of dazzling light—she did see one thing that gave her pause.

Amidst that endless field of corn, there were scarecrows. Dozens of them, crucified on wooden beams; faces made of straw that housed the blackest eyes she'd ever seen. Their bodies were simple, sometimes old sheets that were brown and mottled with time—making them look like monks of an ancient order; but sometimes they wore hand-me-downs. The peculiar part was that each of them had a scythe, the blade of which came up over their shoulders, forming a violent silhouette. It was as if fear and violence had been bred into their very being. Carina had to remind herself that although they were frightening, they were meant to be. And they were doing their job well. She looked around. *No crows,* she thought. She tried to laugh, but when she tried, she kept looking at those ancient, chipped blades and tasting the heavy coating of rust on her throat.

The air smelled of autumn.

CHAPTER SEVEN

CARINA WOKE TO a noise. There were always noises. It was an old house. All old houses were filled with noises. It's as much a part of them as flaked paint and musty smells. But this noise was different. She could've sworn it was something different from any sort of house-sound she'd heard before. Because it was not the sounds of a house.

It was the sound of a man.

She stayed in bed.

She closed her eyes.

She counted to ten.

And she went back to sleep, waking at dawn—feeling better than she had in a long while.

Because now, she was unafraid.

Carina never thought the day would come, but it did, and so soon. Two weeks in the B & B on the outskirts of a little town in Oregon, and she felt refreshed. She hadn't had a single panic attack, although she sometimes felt them bubbling to the surface. But when this bubbling happened, it was easily suppressed. She was happy to be happy.

She'd heard many noises in the last two weeks and Carina knew now that noises were not scary, that noises alone would not hurt her. Each time, it had been a cold wind in the middle of the night, or some sort of humming appliance that reverberated through the floorboards. After a while, it felt silly to check.

The morning light streamed through the windows and she got out of bed. She traipsed tiredly to the kitchen and started her coffee, pulled out some yogurt from the fridge and mixed a spoon of granola into the open container. She read while she ate. The local newspaper, where articles about Larry Dell's Stardust, Miriam

Dell's Craftopia, and a surprising amount of other local stores filled the business pages with superlatives and special sales events. Carina smiled at that; she felt an almost maternal sense of warmth for these characters who lived so large on the pages of their local newspaper. She found it charming that in Greentree the business news had no mention of Wall Street, but a dozen mentions of Larry Dell eliminating late fees for the month of October.

After breakfast, she would exercise. She did a half-hour of yoga and then went out for a half-hour jog. She struggled with it, heaving and huffing by the end, but the burn she felt was ultimately encouraging. It was as if she were reforging herself, inside and out.

Besides lunches with Emily and sparse conversations with Wilbur, she saw little of anyone. She stayed at the house and worked toward continuous improvement of herself and her senses.

Life wasn't always good, but now, it was better.

On a late afternoon, Emily rolled up into the driveway.

"How you doing, girl?" she shouted. Emily had made a game of shouting. Everything was so quiet, she couldn't help but test its limits.

Carina passed through the door, feeling not disheveled, but relaxed. She wore sweatpants and a T-shirt, her hair in a messy bun. "What's up?" she said, her voice absurdly quiet.

Emily would say, "What? What? What?"

And Carina would only lower her voice, until no sound came out, and she only moved her lips. By the end of their game, one was silent and one was screaming at the top of her lungs.

Emily ran up to the porch and hugged Carina. "You look good. Real good."

"Liar."

"I don't lie."

"How's school?"

"Good, the same. Kids get smarter every year. You should see some of their art sometime. I think they're better than I ever was at that age."

"Not exactly a tall order."

"Shut up," she said.

She hadn't had this sort of repartee in years. She was beginning to feel almost normal.

"What's on the menu today?"

Emily smiled. "I was thinking we could go down to Joe's."

"I like Joe's," said Carina.

"And we've got a surprise for you."

"What's that?"

"You'll have to wait and see."

"What am I waiting for?"

"To see it."

Carina shrugged. "Alright, alright. Let me get dressed first."

On the road back to town, which felt further away than it was, even though, in truth, it was only about a mile away, she lost herself staring at the long prairies of corn and the ghostly straw-men that hovered between their rows. *They really are good at their job*, she thought. In her time in the house, she'd almost grown fond of them. Coming into Greentree, she didn't notice them at all, they just faded into the crops and were as invisible as air, but now—once she had seen them—she couldn't stop. They were painted into murals, made into miniatures, even adorned street signs.

"I see you've noticed them," said Emily.

"You're all big Straw-Man fans around here."

"The Wizard of Oz is the newest release we get in Greentree," said Emily.

"So, what's up with all the scarecrows?"

Emily turned downtown. Carina looked for bits of straw and black, obsidian eyes.

"They're sort of like a town mascot, I guess. Larry knows all about that shit. I think Wilbur has a book on Greentree too, it has one on the cover. They might talk about it there."

"Someone wrote a book on Greentree?"

"People write books about anything—why not their podunk town?"

Joe's was a bar and grill that had a line out the door at any hour of the day. Carina wasn't sure how Greentree could sustain this, but there were so few restaurants, it was really no wonder at all. Joe's served good American food for good small town Americans, and that was it. Emily and Carina waited in line and played "spot the scarecrow" while they waited to be seated.

"How many copies of *Children of the Corn* does the Stardust have in stock?"

"That's not a scarecrow movie, silly. But—at least three."

"I'd accept no less."

After a short wait, they were seated by a friendly server who seemed to know Emily intimately, who seemed to know everyone intimately.

Me too, someday, thought Carina.

"You want wine?" asked Emily.

Carina shrugged. "I mean, if you're offering."

"We'll take wine then. Two chardonnays."

Life in Greentree was *different*. Carina had started to become accustomed to it. Wine at noon was not something to fret over. Emily always partook, sometimes having more than one. Sometimes urging Carina to have another too. Each time, they'd laugh themselves silly over old memories, or new ones. Carina would quiz Emily on the ins and outs of Greentree etiquette.

But, as it always did, the conversation turned.

Emily sat up straight. Swallowed. "So, Cari, honestly though—how are you doing?"

"How are you doing?" always meant "How are you doing with Steve?" or "Are you still afraid?"

Carina frowned. "Good enough to want to forget about it."

"Yeah. But you should talk about it."

"Talk about what?"

"He hit you."

"Yeah? What else do you need to hear?"

"He abused you. Emotionally."

"He did," she confirmed. "But now, he's not."

She wished she could articulate how she felt, how Emily's concern was no longer helping. That the continual support was now just excavating the terror and unease she lived with every day for years. But, she couldn't put that into words, because she knew Emily would be quick to dismiss it. She was insistent, positive, and utterly brutal in her quest for the truth.

She stirred her drink. "Well, I just hope you're doing okay. I hope you're okay up there, alone."

"I'm doing fine. I'm doing better when I don't have to think about it though." And that was as close as she got to drawing a line in the sand. She changed the subject. "How is everything with Wilbur?"

"Fine," she said. Emily stared at her drink while Carina

measured her friend's reaction. But, as usual, Emily was tight-lipped and elusive. "He just got promoted at his accounting firm. They've been handing huge bonuses out. They seem to really like him."

"Wow," said Carina, unimpressed but kind. "I'm almost surprised that Greentree even has an accounting firm."

"It's all the small business. People go crazy for them. There are a lot of successful people here." She said that as if it was all she needed to say.

"I could see that. I just don't understand how everything is so successful. It's so remote, there's just not enough customers, right? Or are there?"

Emily smiled thinly. "There must be, right?"

"Yeah, I guess so." Carina thought for a moment. She looked around her and looked at the men and women around them in Joe's. *I think everyone I've met in town has either been well off or the children of those who are well-off.* "Must be something in the water," she said.

———✦———

For one reason or another, Hazel was the highlight of her visits to Emily's home. Wilbur was always kind in a perfunctory sort of way—he'd make comments about the weather, drop hints that he planned to have the B & B occupied by spring, and sometimes talk about his work. Emily would ask if she was okay, tell her that she was there for her as long as she needed, and then try to maintain her facade of perfection.

But Hazel was a lawless, chaotic force and Carina loved her for it.

Her first words to her mother when she asked about her school day? "Fuck you."

To her father, when he told her not to talk to her mother like that: "Fuck you too."

When Carina stood in a doorway that Hazel wanted to get through, she'd say, "Get the fuck out of my way."

She was the single most rebellious girl Carina had ever seen, but there was a dignity to her malevolence. Hazel delighted in making people uncomfortable and therefore always had the high ground. Over the last couple weeks, Carina thought that Hazel was starting to warm up to her—an exciting development in a new life of subdued leisure.

After lunch, Carina once again found herself in a minefield.

Wilbur and Hazel were arguing over nothing, and while Wilbur's face got redder and redder, Hazel only became more playful. She was fencing, sparring—and she was loving it.

"Are you afraid if I go out tonight I'm going to get fucked?"

"Hazel," said Wilbur.

"How hard am I going to get fucked if I go out tonight?"

"Young lady—"

"I might smoke crack too."

"You're not going anywhere."

"I think I'm just going to go."

And she left, just like that. Hazel wouldn't have taken an inch of shit from Steve Calico.

Through gritted-teeth, in that *I know we have a guest, honey* voice, he said, "Are you going to go after her?"

And then, through similarly gritted teeth, Emily responded: "I think she'll be fine, dear."

Wilbur threw up his hands and left the room. His footsteps thundered through the house.

"It's okay," said Emily, still obviously furious. "She just wants to hang out with her friends. She's at that age."

"Of course. We were all like that," said Carina.

Inside, she cheered at Emily's dismay. *She's done so much for me*, she thought, coaching her way through her emotions. But, as Emily put her head into her hands and rubbed her eyes, Carina still savored her schadenfreude. Sometimes, she realized, you just need to see the cracks.

And as well hidden as they were, there were always cracks.

"You said something about a surprise?"

Emily looked up. She blinked the beginnings of her tears away. Her voice changed, her tone lightened. "Yes, of course, of course. Yes, a surprise. I almost forgot. Sorry—sorry about that. Wilbur, honey?"

Wilbur popped back into the living room, still agitated but somewhat settled. "Are you going after her?"

"No, no—Carina. The—you know, thing. Can we give it to her now?"

This also seemed to mollify Wilbur, a welcome distraction.

"Oh, yeah. Of course. I nearly forgot. Yeah, yeah, yeah." He spoke to himself and grabbed his keys from a wooden hook on the wall. "Let's go outside."

Emily pushed her along. "Go ahead now, let's take a look."

Carina went outside with her benefactors, feeling confused, excited, and somewhat dreading what charity they'd decided to bestow upon her today.

"We thought this might be good for you, Carina. Not to push you or anything, but Wilbur thought—"

Wilbur cleared his voice. "We're happy to have you here, and the house is yours until spring. Don't think we're trying to push you along. But it's a ways out there, and hard to get around."

Carina was staring at a car. Not a new one. But one that had probably been collecting dust in the Mueller's garage.

"We thought this might give you some more freedom, for the time being."

Carina turned to her friends. "Thank you," she said. "Thank you."

Wilbur waved it off. "It's Em's old car, we weren't using it. But now, if you wanted to get a job—"

Emily slapped her husband's stomach playfully. "Stop it," she said.

"No, I think that'll be a good idea." She didn't understand the words coming out of her mouth but they came anyway. She realized earlier, she hadn't been joking about it. She needed *something*. "I need to start getting back on my feet."

Wilbur forced the key off his keychain and tossed it to her. She caught it in mid-air, effortlessly.

"Alright," he said, "you got wheels."

CHAPTER EIGHT

CARINA STARED OUT into the blackness of her room.
She listened.

Clop.

She had chosen one of the rooms on the second story because she thought it'd give her some sense of solace, some inner peace. Being closer to God and all of that. She also liked the view in the morning. She'd wake up, look out across the sea of golden, dying corn and see the sun glittering off the gilded dew of their leaves. From that view, the fields went forever, and the treeline that held Greentree captive was forever away. The scarecrows felt like humble journeymen this way—humble breakfast companions to her morning ritual of coffee and a book.

But now, she held the covers, her eyes tightly shut. It was different at night.

A noise, a creaking; perhaps a footstep.

What was that?

Then: a repetition of that noise. A stilted gait. Walking.

Oh God, someone's here.

Clop, clop, clop, clop.

The sound of heavy boots.

Carina heard them, coming up the stairs.

Clop, clop, clop, clop.

Slow, methodical. As if the person those heavy steps belonged to was in no hurry.

I'm okay. I'm fixed now. This isn't panic, this is real!

It was true. The noises were real and she could hear them creaking up the stairs and to her door. There was nothing imaginary about this.

She swallowed.

Carina opened the drawer to her nightstand. She felt around inside it, searching for the wooden handle.

Yes!

She held the knife in the dark, pointing it to the closed door.

Clop, clop, clop, clop.

The noise was louder, right on the other side of the door. It was right there! Carina's muscles froze. She couldn't move.

Oh God, it's going to happen again. She tried to breathe but—

She wasn't the only one breathing.

Soft breaths, right on the other side of her door.

Someone was there, right on the other side. Breathing. And Carina knew the moment they walked in, she'd be helpless. She'd never stabbed anyone before. She'd never been in a fight.

I'm going to die. I'm going to die, she thought.

And then, outside: a gust of wind, loud and horrible like the sound of eternity itself. Ghosts wailed against the window pane beside her bed.

The door opened.

Just a crack.

The hinges squealed.

She sat up, holding the knife so tight that sweat had wet the handle.

I've got to get up, she thought. *I've got to fight.*

She cried angrily. *No! No! No! I was supposed to be safe!*

The wind howled again and she forced her body up—*now or never, ride or die, live for the glory of dying in battle*—and she flung her nervous body to the door. The wind screamed. She thrashed, chopping into the dark. She was a wild woman, a tornado. And when she got to the door she slid her hand across the wall and hit the lights, and then in one movement, swung her knife into the black sliver and flung it open with her other hand.

She leaned into the hallway, the kitchen knife slicing air.

Her body relaxed.

"Thank God," she said to no one.

The hall was empty. The stairs were untouched. The house creaked with cold autumn winds.

⤙⤚

There were not any marks on the wood of the stairs to suggest that someone had been in the house. Carina walked the path carefully and cautiously, afraid of what she would find. But, as she suspected, it was nothing. Only nerves.

But it wasn't, right?

The house looked as it always did, a tribute to modern rustic affluence.

She held her arms close to her. She didn't feel like jogging any more. She told herself it was because it was getting colder. Or maybe it was because of Larry Dell.

Just as he said, he was more than happy to take her on at the Stardust.

Maybe that's it, she rationalized—work anxiety. The vacation was over. Questions from the future had come fast and hard.

How am I going to get an apartment come spring? Where will I go? Who will I be?

She showered, taking care to neatly style her hair. She wore a pair of khakis and a teal polo.

"It'll be great," he said with a big, capped-tooth smile. "This is as Greentree as it gets."

She got into the car and drove, surprisingly nervous, taking each curve in the road as if it were especially treacherous.

When she arrived, there were two other cars in the parking lot, both sputtering clouds in the cold morning as their drivers sat and waited for the store to open. She waited too.

Eventually, Larry Dell extricated himself from his vehicle and walked to the door, and just a step behind him, a young girl with a blonde ponytail bounced from another vehicle behind him. Carina cut the ignition and got out as well.

"Looks like we have a new hire," said Larry.

The girl, no older than seventeen, stretched out a hand to Carina. "Hi, I'm Jessica."

"Carina."

"Pretty name," she said.

"Thank you."

"Go ahead and show Carina how we open, give her the grand tour. She's going to be helping out here for a while."

"Right-o, Mr. Dell."

The girl enthusiastically showed her the store. *Can a place be unstuck in time?* wondered Carina. The Stardust was an anachronism, and yet here it was—thriving. The return box of movies was filled to the brim. New DVD cases were ready to have Stardust stickers applied to their top right corner. Candy needed to be stocked. As Jessica took her behind the counter, she realized that the Stardust felt more like a replica than anything else. As if someone had rebuilt a memory to exact specifications.

"Here's the cash register and you can look up anyone you want here, that's the cool thing. And over here, are the movies, of course. What's your favorite?"

"Movie?"

"Yeah, everyone's got a favorite movie."

"I don't know if I have a favorite. I like older movies, I guess. Classics. *The Maltese Falcon.*"

The girl nodded in recognition. "We watched that one in school! That's a good one, a little hard to follow though."

Carina hadn't the experience working with young people, but she knew she was supposed to ask questions back. "What's yours?"

"Oh, that's easy. I love the new *Mad Max.* It's, like, totally badass."

She led her through the sections. "This is Action, where I always go. Over here is drama—boring. Horror is over here. And then we have some Classics over here, not a lot though—want me to put in a good word with Mr. Dell so we can get some more of your favorites?"

"I think it'll be okay."

"And then we have Romance, Sci-fi, and New Releases are all along that back wall."

Carina eyes followed along, drinking in the colorful covers. Her eyes paused, just for a moment, on the curtain that parted the selection.

If Jessica noticed, she didn't let on. She continued the tour, leaving Carina breathless from the pace.

"Really, the most important part is scanning in the returned movies and then getting them back out on the shelf, so our customers can rent them!"

Carina felt uneasy around the girl, her relentless bubbliness overwhelmed her. She was permanently wired and fiercely proud of her job.

For most of the day, Larry Dell stayed in his office in the back, only coming out to inform Carina that "she was doing great."

Sometimes he would chat with customers, but Carina got the sense that he didn't come out unless there was someone who would see him. At the Stardust, he was a movie star in his own right.

Halfway through the shift, Jessica informed her she would be leaving. "You just got to hold it down for a half hour and the next shift will be in! I know you can do it."

"Of course, sure, no problem." She felt strange being so submissive to a child, but Jessica *was* technically her boss.

Nearly alone in the store, she wandered the aisles, looking at films. There were no customers in the middle of the day, but every once in a while she could hear Larry Dell tapping on his keyboard in the back. Her eyes wandered back and forth across the store. Nothing to do, nothing to see.

But, they weren't really wandering. Not really.

They kept going back to the same thing.

The beaded curtain, with "Adults Only" written above it in construction paper.

Carina had seen pornography, of course. Steve used to show it to her on his phone. She was unmoved by it, by the hulking men and screaming women—it seemed something uncanny and unnatural, not the product of humans but humanoids. Sometimes, she thought Steve enjoyed it because he couldn't tell the difference.

She stood up and took several glancing walks around the store. It was as if she were fencing with the idea in real time. She thrusted, parried, and riposted with the idea until she eventually found herself staring at the beaded curtain. She ran her hands along them. They rattled, smooth and furious, fighting to show her what they hid.

Within a moment, she was on the other side.

It might as well have been a whole other world.

Is this still Greentree? she thought.

Of course it is, silly. There's scarecrows.

The room was small, not much more than a closet, really. But, it had been intricately painted. On the back wall was a mural that wrapped around all three walls. A great scarecrow surrounded by stalks of yellow corn and a blood red sky. Carina had the sudden sensation that she was not where she was supposed to be, that despite being an adult and an employee, that this was a place where she was not allowed. And then there were the discs.

They stared back at her, unmarked mirrors in thin plastic jewel cases. Four shelves, on three walls, facing out—capturing her tight lips and wide eyes in a distorted, rainbow reflection.

She backed away. The beads swallowed her.

Why aren't they marked? Why aren't there barcodes? Why don't they have titles or pictures or—

The door chime rang and she jumped.

She swiveled around, holding her hand to her heart. Self-consciously, she heard the beads swaying behind her with their insidious rattle.

Something to do. Something to look busy. Her hands snapped out in front of her to the closest thing.

She pretended to be organizing an end-cap display of science-fiction classics.

Hazel Mueller, dressed in black from head to toe, looked up from her phone and grimaced. "You work here now?"

"Just started today."

Hazel rolled her eyes. "Fine. Do you know what to do?"

"A little, I'm still learning."

Hazel shrugged. She seemed to take this as a reasonable answer. She relaxed. "Is Larry here?"

"Yeah, he's in his office."

"Cool." She went into the center of the store and puffed out her chest, arching her back, and then bellowing: "Good afternoon, Mr. Dell!"

Carina smiled and from the back office, slightly muffled, she heard a weary, "Good afternoon, Hazel."

"He loves me," she said matter-of-factly, and seeing that Carina was smiling made her smile too.

Chapter Nine

THE STARDUST WAS becoming a second home. It was not as decidedly homey as the one made up for her surrounded by the corn and the trees and the scarecrows, but it did have its charms. For the first time, Carina felt like she was part of something, a community. It was now the end of September, and in only a month and a half, her past life seemed like a vision from another's dream.

She was working with Hazel, who she looked forward to seeing the most out of all the teenage girls she worked with. Hazel would lean on the counters, harass Larry, and generally be a disaffected, bad influence—but she always had something to say.

"I'm pretty sure Mom hates Dad," she said one day.

"Why do you think that? They seem happy to me."

Hazel scoffed. "C'mon, you're not that fucking dumb."

"I'm not?"

"No, you're not. You can see it with your own eyes, right? *I* think she wants to divorce him."

"Do you think she will?"

"Probably not."

"Why not?"

"Because she's addicted to her seat at the Ivory Tower."

"Is there an Ivory Tower in Greentree?"

Hazel looked at her with mocking eyes. "Are you fucking kidding me? You're standing in it."

"The Stardust?"

"No, not just the Stardust. But, like, everything here. Greentree is preppy as fuck. Even being a teacher, you can actually make bank here because you're considered a community pillar."

"Is that right?" Carina laughed. "So you're Mom's just chasing status?"

"Of course she is and she doesn't care that Dad's an asshole."

"Why is he an asshole? He seems fine to me, I've known some real assholes."

"He's an asshole because he's just like her, but better at it. He's already a member of the Knights of Commerce—our dumb little club for business owners."

Carina shrugged. "I can't blame them for being proud of what they have. I'm lucky I'm here at all."

"Ugh, that's the other thing." Hazel spoke the words with exaggerated disdain. "*You.*"

Carina knew not to take her recriminations too seriously. She quite openly had a bone to pick with everyone. "Oh, and what did I do?"

"You didn't do anything, it's what you represent to Mom. She thinks she can symbolically break up with Dad by keeping you here because you left your husband. It's some weird Jungian shit."

"You think she wants to use me as an example?"

"More like an icon or something."

Carina had considered the thought before, but was mostly concerned as to how much Hazel knew about her. *Did Emily tell her about Steve?*

"They're all bourgeoisie dicks anyways. When I get older, I'm either moving out or molotoving all this bullshit."

"I actually really like it here," said Carina, scanning in the returned DVDs. "It's a lot better than where I used to live. It feels safer too."

Hazel scoffed. "What's the date?"

"The twenty-fifth."

"Give it a couple of days."

"What do you mean by that?"

"Oh yeah, I forgot you didn't know anything." Hazel shook her head. "Just bullshit stories we tell each other for a laugh, me and the kids at school."

"Please, do share."

Hazel rolled her eyes. "You're so annoying."

"Yeah. I know. But you like me anyways. I'm an icon, remember?"

"It's bullshit, but we always joke about the Autumn Autopsies."

"What's that?"

"Yeah, around this time every year someone usually dies. It's big news around here, because there's not that many people. But there's always jokes and shit. Rumors."

"That it's a sacrifice? Like a cult thing?"

"Well, yeah. We all joke about cult shit here. Because, living in this town is like living in a fucking cult!" She yelled it so Larry Dell could hear it.

From the far back: "Watch your language, please."

Hazel banged her head on the counter. "Rich boring bastards think they can do anything they want," she said. "Probably because they can."

Later that night, she was at the Mueller's, where they talked about the banalities of country living while also trading barbs with their daughter. In time, Carina began to think she knew Hazel better than she knew her parents, but that was only because of the Stardust. Wilbur bristled at nearly everything his daughter said, but it was so performatively genial that it felt like a mask. Emily nodded with tight-lipped and dismissive *yes dears* that betrayed the fact that they considered Hazel nothing more than a girl who likes to act out. A teenager.

"She's just at that age," one of them said for the hundredth time that night.

And Carina agreed, once again saying that, "Yes, I was there too, at one point or another."

While she could chalk up the intensity of Hazel's hatred of her parents to hormones, she could also see how frustrating it must be to never be heard or seen as anything but a biological machine lashing out. She was seen as a vessel for necessary but irritating angst, and disregarded for it too.

Steve had seen Carina much the same way.

But once things settled down and Hazel plugged in her earbuds and sat in the corner reading on her phone, Wilbur and Emily relaxed and conversation began in earnest. The usual Greentree topics were brought up. Wilbur talked about his accounting business. Emily said that she was up for a teaching award. And Carina admitted that work wasn't too bad and that she enjoyed Hazel's company.

"You don't have to say that," said Emily, embarrassed. "You shouldn't be working in the first place."

"I'm fine and Hazel is a delight. I've met worse."

Wilbur licked his teeth and ran a hand through his thinning hair. The conversation stalled. Finally, he said, "Say, we were wondering if you'd be interested in going to a local party with us?"

Carina shrugged. "What kind of party?"

"It's the biggest bash in Greentree. Everyone who's anyone will be there."

"Pillars of the community?"

She could tell Hazel didn't have any music playing and was listening intently because she smiled at that.

"Yes, actually," said Wilbur.

"It's just a local gathering for business owners and such—great for networking and all that."

"Good food and drink too."

"What do you say?"

Hazel made a cutting motion across her neck, from where her parents couldn't see. Carina smiled, even though she found it disturbing. "Sure," she said, trying to ignore Hazel's death throes in the background. "It'd be my pleasure."

Carina grew fonder of the scarecrows every twilight. She sat on her porch and drank sweet coffee with a little rum, her hands warm on the mug, and watched the sunset with her straw comrades. She worked now, just like them. In this, she found within herself a new compatibility with Greentree. She worked. She exchanged labor for money. And the scarecrows out in the field, their black edges all the blacker against the bloody sky, worked too. She admired their rusty blades, their shapeless hats, their sunken black eyes—they were the expression of workers who had been working forever.

Chapter Ten

TOWN SEEMS LIKE *a shithole. Too small. Too weird. Too much of nothing.*

Steve Calico arrived in Greentree at night. He'd been driving for a week and hated every second of it. His ass was sticking to the driver's seat. The car smelled like farts and snack food and he'd only needed to ask for directions three times, which he took as a pretty good sign. Shouldn't be too many witnesses along the way.

Witnesses to what?

Steve entered Greentree without any thought or purpose. He wasn't sure what he was going to do, only sure that whatever it was, he would end up doing it. Carina leaving had wounded him. It was a deep cut—one that he never considered himself to be susceptible to. The Running Woman of yore. The Angry Man. He went to her the same way birds follow magnetic fields. It was part of his DNA, the elegance of his design. He was the Angry Man and he would have to chase the Running Woman. And when he caught her?

He didn't know. But he'd had time to weigh many options.

Welcome to Greentree!

He saw the sign and nodded gravely, as if it were the validation he needed the whole time. Yes, I'm here. I did it. I found her.

He put the car in park and went into the gas station. He selected some jerky, some beer, and a couple bags of chips.

"How you doing tonight, lad?"

He liked to say lad now, it was an affectation he'd been trying out since he hit North Dakota. It always seemed to get a reaction. The kid on the other side of the counter gave him what he wanted, a smirk.

"I'm fine, tired," said the kid. "Late shift."

Steve whistled. "They get close to killing you with those, huh?"

"That's right. Tired all the time."

"When do you get off?"

"Five in the AM."

"Well, ain't that some bullshit."

"You're telling me, bud. Is that all for you?"

"Yeah, yeah—that's about it for me. Just need some supplies. Say though, you know Greentree pretty well? I'm new here."

"Lived here all my life."

Steve leaned in. "So, I don't know what kind of place this is— but would you say it's pretty chill, with some comings and goings, if you know what I mean? Are there any places that would be, maybe, more discreet than others?"

The kid's smirk turned to confusion. "I'm not sure I know what you mean. You need a place to stay?"

Steve gave up. "Yeah, for a couple of nights. But, I don't know— call me private. I don't like it when people are getting into my business, if you know what I'm saying."

"Sure," he said and looked up as he thought. "I know the Mueller's have a bed and breakfast on the outskirts of town, but I don't think it's open yet."

Mueller. Where did he hear that before? "Anywhere else?"

"Yeah, but just one. Real small, but cozy, I hear. Lot of kids . . . " The cashier's cheeks went red.

Steve let his smile grow long and wolfish. "Oh yeah?"

"You can bet it's booked full after every prom."

"Well, wouldn't you know? You mind giving me directions so I can drink this here beer and listen to your local hooligans fuck each other's brains out?"

The kid laughed. "Yeah, man. Of course." And he reached over for a piece of scratch paper and a pen. He scribbled it out in boxy letters and Steve leaned in close and nodded along, making sure the kid knew he was hanging on his every word. On the way out, carefully studying the instructions, he asked the kid his name.

"Glad to meet you, Jason," he said.

He left the gas station, flustered. His hands held the note and he kept looking at it. Because something was wrong. Not with the note. But the whole thing. Why didn't he feel good? Steve Calico, when he had to, had a nearly endless well of charm and when the situation called for it, and sometimes when it didn't, he loved to see his own effect on people. He'd charmed the kid's ass off. He should be happy now, he should be feeling on top of the world. Another point for Steve Calico.

But, he didn't.

He took the directions and tried to ignore the feeling. To somehow stay focused. He found the motel, a one-story affair with maybe twenty rooms total, arranged in a big bracket shape. The sign had been freshly painted out front and it looked quite a bit nicer than the kid made it seem.

At the front desk counter, the service was kind and personable. It was a young woman, pretty, and normally, he would've made a repeat of the act he did with Jason but he couldn't bring it out of himself. He was distracted.

When she gave him the room key he only nodded and said, "Thank you, thank you," repeating himself like a nervous child.

He laid in the motel bed and cracked open a beer and thought. He turned on the television. Lights and colors screamed as he flipped through channels and convinced himself nothing was wrong. His eyes wandered from the TV to his surroundings. The motel room was decorated with motel art—a framed painting of a straw-man sitting beside a pumpkin.

Some po-dunk shit. Why did Carina even come here, anyways?

He'd never heard of Greentree, Oregon. But it only took a little digging to find out where she was going. A friend of a friend talks too much. A sob story to her landlord about how she's trying to take his kids. *She's off the rails and I'm afraid she's gonna hurt 'em. She's not normal when she's using.* And they gave him what he needed. And so he went to Greentree.

But why?

He finished off a can of beer and crumpled it in his hand. The beer can fell lightly to the floor.

Mueller.

He smiled. *Oh shit.*

A puzzle piece fell into place.

He stood up, finishing the next beer off in one long chug.

A vivid memory.

Emily.

He'd met her once or twice many years ago, just a little before she got pregnant and married that accountant. It was back when he and Carina were newlyweds. He had to shake hands and smile and try to charm them, and he hated that, because they weren't shit. Steve didn't like the prospect of charming people who condescended to his company. He was a factory line worker back then and Emily and what's-his-face were going to run off and be very well-off and la-di-da.

"They're assholes," he told Carina. He swallowed and turned to steel.

"What? What's wrong? Em's my friend—is something wrong?"

He'd felt emasculated, de-balled in just one dinner date. Cut down to nothing. They were buying a house. They were going to move up to Maine, then they were going to Florida. They were always moving. They were gonna go to Europe for a while too. Just remembering it all made him want to snap. Almost twenty years later, he'd almost forgotten about it all, and he'd been a helluva lot happier too.

That bitch just couldn't stand being with a guy like me. Yeah, she had a story all worked out, didn't she? Made a real good resume. Daughter of immigrants. University scholarship. Art Major.

He spat on the floor.

But he remembered the name. Mueller. Just a moment, a cringing moment he couldn't let go of even years later.

They were at the dinner table and everyone else was dressed to the nines. Carina didn't tell him it was going to be a nice place, and he would've worn something else if he knew.

"You're fine, man. You're fine. These places don't really give a shit about that sort of thing," said what's-his-name.

"Yes, but someone should've told me."

Carina fumbled, trying to change the subject when she felt his eyes on her. *Good*, he thought.

"So," she said, manufacturing excitement, "are you going to change your name?"

Emily smiled and said, "Say hello to the new Mrs. Mueller."

And it was at the point where Steve Calico laughed. "Mueller," he said.

"That's the name," said what's-his-name. And in that moment, it was as if Steve was an ant beneath his dress shoe.

He looked up to realize that the whole table was staring at him.

It was a funny name, he thought, panicked. *It was just a funny sounding name.*

Carina had to look away, the embarrassment was too much. She poked at the food on her plate and he could see her teeth grinding beneath her cheeks, waiting anxiously for the moment to pass.

He hated that the most.

He hated feeling like the fool.

"Sorry," he said weakly. "My name's Calico, I don't have room to talk."

Even years later, now, on the motel bed, he wished he could take that apology back.

And now, two decades later, maybe he would.

"Mueller," he said. He opened his mouth like a swallowing void and laughed. "Mueller! Mueller! Mueller!"

CHAPTER ELEVEN

"You DIDN'T TELL me that the party was here."

"We were very relieved when you said yes."

Lights had been strung up on poles around her house—or as she was more aware than ever, the Mueller's Bed and Breakfast. She nodded her way through the proceedings, forcing a smile and reminding herself, *this is not my home.*

And that was fine.

"We're sorry though," said Emily. "When we invited you, we forgot we made this commitment. It's a big thing and at the time, we had a place to make it work, so we just sort of . . . double-booked."

Carina poured herself a glass of punch. "It's fine with me. I don't have any room to complain. Not my house, right?"

Emily put a hand on her arm. "Just because it's not your house doesn't mean you're not welcome."

She returned the touch. "I know." She changed the subject. "How's Wilbur? He seems stressed."

Wilbur was trying to erect a table, cursing as it continually collapsed.

"It's a big day, I suppose. That's what they all say anyways."

"What do you mean: they all? Aren't you one of them?"

You are a pillar, aren't you?

Emily arched an eyebrow. "I'm just along for the ride, this is Wilbur's thing."

"Oh, okay."

"God fucking dammit!" screamed Wilbur. "Honey, can you—?"

Emily sighed. "I better . . . "

"Yes, please. Go."

Carina watched Emily go over to him, to help him with the

table, which he accepted somewhat gracefully. When she had it together, he muttered something about her having smaller hands, then went on muttering that it was a big night.

The air was cool but comfortable. The Mueller's had big outdoor heaters in place as well as an outdoor bar and bartender. Carina tried to stay out of the way, but when the guests began to arrive, Emily was pulling her around, from group to group, introducing her in turn while also introducing herself. She didn't recognize any of them but Larry.

"Are you enjoying the festivities?" he asked.

The men around her were much like him, in their 50s, with taut white skin and immaculate teeth. They all stared at her expectantly.

"Yes, very much so. It's a lovely place."

"Well, it only gets better from here. Eventually, Emily here will have to bring out her sangria."

Emily laughed. "I know my cue when I hear it. It's in the fridge. One moment."

Carina nodded to the men and followed Emily, eager to have a reason to depart. "You're a good hostess," she said, searching for something to say.

"Just another fool in Greentree's court." Emily produced a pitcher from the fridge. "What Larry wants, Larry gets."

Carina snorted. She liked seeing Emily like this, a hint of that vindictiveness she left behind her. A taste of the wicked.

When they arrived with the pitcher, they were swept up again. Carina's body tensed, her heart beat fast.

No, not right now. Not today. Please.

She breathed through grinding teeth and focused outward. She tried to be nice, if not interesting, at least interested.

Carina realized that while Wilbur quickly found his way in with a group of men that seemed to know him, drinking tall glasses of beer and laughing near where the grass met the corn—everyone seemed to be at a loss for Emily's identity. They needed reminders. *Oh, where did we meet? Was that back at the old school? What class do you teach? Yes, I think I might recognize you, it's hard when you meet so many people.* Each time though, Emily accepted their disinterest with aplomb, sweetly answering their questions and introducing Carina as the current tenant of the farmhouse behind them.

"Beautiful home," they'd say, and then turn back to the people they knew.

In reality, there were only about fifty people at the party. Most of them were wealthy in a drab, dressed down sort of way. They wore ugly jeans and polos tucked in over their guts. Some of the women wore sweaters and thick leggings. All of them, together, formed a collage of the ugly upper class. They drank yellow lagers and threw back shots of twenty-dollar vodka. They prided themselves on their motorcycles and cable packages. They lived in large manufactured homes that were spacious and identical to each other. If one were to ask them what they did, they'd smugly smile and say, "I'm a business owner."

And in Greentree, that was enough. These were the bourgeoisie that Hazel referred to with a cutting tone. They were the same ones her mother danced for, begging for approval; the same that her father disappeared into, effortlessly. She wished Hazel was here, actually. She would've liked to hear her commentary on the whole affair.

But, it was better that she was not.

As the night went along, everyone got drunker. Even Emily, who so often remained poised, became looser and looser.

"Cari, I'm fucking wasted."

"I see that."

She was hanging onto the counter in the kitchen. She had been sent on a mission—to retrieve more ice. Somewhere between the front lawn and the kitchen she started to fall into things, to hold onto them, as if they were going to wisp away the moment she ceased her touch. The walls, the house, Wilbur, her drink, and Carina. She grabbed onto all of them on the way to the fridge, all the while mourning her lost sobriety.

Carina helped her with the ice and followed her out to the minibar, where she dumped it into a cooler of cheap beer. "There," she said. "All done . . . no problem."

"You did it," said Carina, holding her friend. "I haven't seen you like this since college."

"I haven't been like this since then," she slurred. "I only had a couple."

"Sure."

"Why . . . aren't *you* drinking?"

"I have work in the morning."

"Oh, *p-shaw*."

"It's the truth," she said simply.

Emily laid her head on her shoulder. "You were always too good for this world . . . too good for—"

"Nope. Don't say his name."

"Okay," she said, closing her eyes. She stayed like that for a moment. They were both on the porch and the sun had set. Carina was drinking sparkling water and Emily had given up on dancing for her rich friends.

Over by the corn, Wilbur called to his wife. "Em, we're going for a walk! You coming?"

She blinked, sleepily, raising her head. "Walk?"

"Wilbur wants to know if you want to go with him and the others."

There were about seven of them, Larry Dell included, all holding their beers. If it weren't for the tiki lights, she wouldn't have been able to see them at all.

"What are they holding?"

She could barely make it out, but for the orange flickering shadows. Larry was holding a small . . . something.

"Probably more booze," she said, not allowing her to answer. She stood up on liquid legs. "Alright, boys," she yelled. "I'm coming."

"Where are you going to go?" She didn't mean to sound wounded, but she didn't want to be left all alone either.

"Oh, just taking a mosey about the rows." She leaned in, quiet, whispering. "This is where business gets done at these things." She winked. "Wilbur says this is where business gets done."

"Are you gonna be alright?"

"Oh sure, fine. Yeah, I'll be fine." She walked carefully in the way that drunk people do when they're desperately trying to appeal against their current state. One foot in front of the other, hips and shoulder square, arms loose and head lolling.

"Okay, bye," said Carina, half-heartedly. She watched them disappear into the corn.

———

Carina was talking to a local couple about movies when she heard the scream. That's all anyone seemed to want to talk about with her.

She was the only one to hear it at first.

"What was that?"

"Might be a crow squawking."

"That wasn't a crow."

She knew that, because there were never any birds.

The scream sounded again, sharp and pained.

"Sounds like a woman," she said.

It was coming from the corn.

Her heart thumped in her chest. She closed her eyes for a split second and tried to imagine what the *person who would know what to do* would do. She opened her eyes. "Does anyone have a flashlight?"

Others were starting to turn their heads, albeit slowly, as if the blood-curdling scream from the corn was an annoyance more than an emergency.

"A flashlight! We need a flashlight!" she called out across the lawn.

She broke away from the old man and woman who seemed more confused than terrified and started to make her way to the corn. *I can use my phone if I have to.*

Finally, someone said, "I got one in my trunk, just a second."

If I knew what I was doing, what would I do now?

"Is anyone here a doctor?"

An older man raised his hand. "Guilty," he said. He walked over to her with a half-smile. "Might as well have a look, eh?"

A young man came back with a flashlight and the three pushed through the corn rows.

"I think it came from over there," said Carina, pointing. She felt ridiculous, leading two uninterested men into a corn field.

They moved among the rows, their feet crunching, the sky black above them. The doctor yawned, cursed under his breath. The young man with the flashlight lacked urgency with his sweeping illuminations of the corn.

"I haven't heard anything for a while," he said.

"It was probably nothing," said the doctor. "Just the call of the wild."

"A coyote yelping, perhaps," said the young man.

"There's good food, drink—"

They froze, each holding their breath. The rustling sound of corn husks.

Carina listened closely. She had to focus not to hear her heartbeat.

Footsteps.

Heavy, plodding footsteps.

"Hello, is everything alright?" called the doctor.

They waited for an answer.

Silence.

"It was probably the wind," said the young man.

"No, it wasn't the wind."

Carina pulled out her phone. "Let me call her."

"Who?"

"Emily."

"Emily?"

"Wilbur's wife," said the young man.

"Ah yes, good man, that one," said the doctor in the dark.

She shook her head, frustrated that no one else seemed to be terrified. They were steady and bored and—

The chiming of a phone.

The young man flashed his light in the direction it came from, into the deeper darkness of the corn.

"She's over there."

They marched on wordlessly.

Carina's palms were sweating and she remembered that time in the supermarket. She clenched her teeth and tears welled up in her eyes and she thought, *oh god, oh god, just once let me be the hero*.

And that's when she reached a hand out to touch something familiar.

A post. She'd seen them all the time, in the daylight, but never touched one.

Sometimes, when Carina was feeling blasphemous, she called them crucifixes. She put her hand on the post now, and dark clouds parted; silver light illuminated the field. She turned her head to see another one of the ancient crucified straw-men and her breath hitched.

Nothing.

The spot was empty.

* * *

Steve Calico left his car down the twisting road. He was a little drunk, he'd have to admit, but not enough to be wobbly. Just brave. He'd found the house easy enough and he'd gone far enough past it to not make a scene. He didn't want to be noticed and even now, after traveling cross country, he wasn't sure he actually wanted to do anything. But still, he was here. He parked his car and grabbed two choice items from his trunk—a gun and some rope.

Well, I wasn't planning on doing anything sinister, officer. Just wanted to scare her. This woman—No, this bitch, tried to just up and leave me. Can you believe that? He practiced the lines in his head but nothing sounded right. Eventually, he gave up.

I guess I'll just have to not get caught.

The corn parted ways for him, he dipped in and out of rows. He thought of how as a kid, his dad would take him camping. He taught him to follow the stars, skin a deer—stuff most of the other city kids didn't know about. This place might not be so bad after all. He breathed deep, smelling sweet manure, dead leaves, and crisp Autumn air. He felt less caged out here, freer than he'd ever been.

They were having a party. It was a blip of light in the middle of nowhere. Nothing more than a modest glow and in it were only a couple dozen people, mulling about in the backyard that might as well have been a field, drinking and talking.

He wasn't sure if Carina was there, but he'd promised himself that if she was, there'd be hell to pay. The idea that his wife had moved across the country, out of their shitty apartment, all the way to Bumfuck, Oregon, and managed to get herself a mansion and a bunch of rich friends upset him deeply.

His eyes adjusted in the moonlight.

He wasn't prepared for the quiet.

There was a party over there, probably not more than a quarter mile from him, but any noise was swallowed up by that huge void of the sky.

But also, it was the wrong kind of silence.

It wasn't quiet. There was quiet, but it wasn't quiet as he knew it. There were endless rustlings, strange noises, footsteps—he was sure he heard footsteps—and all of them kept moving. He heard the scratching of vegetation. And it was in one place, then another. But in between each individual noise, and they were all distinct and separate, there was an infinite void of nothing. A screaming nothingness that was as hard to ignore as the orchestra of rustlings.

He pushed deeper into the corn though, his old pistol heavy in his hand.

I'm making too much noise, he thought.

His steps were thunderous, too much crunch for a smart tracker.

He stopped, listened.

Those fucking footsteps.

He turned his head and listened. *Where the fuck are you?*

The footsteps continued.

Corn stalks pushed each other in the wind, creating a resounding chorus of organic static.

There was something out here, he was sure of it.

He got low to the ground and army crawled forward, his gun tucked into the back of his jeans. He felt the ground wriggle underneath him, wet with worms and cow shit, probably. He almost gagged, almost screamed at the wriggling, but bit the inside of his cheeks until the urge passed.

Okay, fine. Good. Moving on.

He kept crawling. Then, suddenly, stopped. He was getting closer to the party, he thought. He heard voices.

"You know, we're really not supposed to go into the corn," said the doctor.

Carina held a hand up, slipping into her new role. "Shh," she said. "I hear someone."

The Doctor paid her no mind. "It's dangerous out here, especially if you think something . . . untoward is happening."

"He's right, you know. They probably just fell down, drunk. They'll wake up and find their way back. Happens all the time." The young man turned the flashlight to mimic her eye line. "I think we should go back."

Carina shook her head. "I hear something. I think we might be close."

The flashlight illuminated a hint of it, its shape, traipsing confidently through the corn. She inhaled slowly, controlled. She was trying to be in control.

"There," she whispered.

It vanished between rows. But for the second she saw it, she was sure it was a man. Or, well—

She had to laugh. Because it didn't seem real.

"You saw that, right?"

"What?"

"Where?"

She stopped. "This must be a joke." She turned to the other men. "Is this a prank?"

They looked at her with serious eyes. "What did you see?"

Carina turned back toward the rows of corn, puzzled. She didn't want to say it.

He was covered in mud and very close.

He was so goddamned close. He could smell the bitch. He could smell the men.

What the fuck is wrong with this place?

Who the fuck are these people?

They couldn't see him, thank fuck. He'd been careful, quiet. No one knew shit about where he was because he'd been careful not to let them. He was good like that, being so quiet and careful and all. But now, he was thinking about high-tailing it out of there, middle fingers to the wind.

They were filming her.

Not Carina. It would've been okay if it had been Carina, somehow. She deserved what she got.

But this?

He tried to make sense of it all.

She was nude, her clothes in a pile on the ground. Her head rolled back and forth and she seemed out of her mind. The men around her were talking, nervously, or maybe excitedly—and the woman was tied to a post. A work lamp lit their space and one of them, perhaps the most fervent of the supporters, held a small camcorder on the woman.

Steve Calico didn't dare move a muscle.

A man with a ponytail covered his eyes. He wasn't looking at her, in fact, he was trying not to. "Are you sure?" he asked.

One of the other men put a hand on his back, patted him. "It'll be alright, Wil. It'll be alright. Whatever you need, time away, help with the youngin'—we'll have you."

"It's just—" He sobbed.

"I know, we know. It's never easy."

The man with the camcorder hovered close to her nude body with a voyeur's delight. "She's a hot one," he said. "I know this isn't the right time to say this, Wil—but goddamn."

The sad man, Wil, laughed despite himself. "She's pretty, alright."

"That just makes it all the better, you know?"

"Does it?"

"Oh yeah," he said, as if that explained everything. "What happens out here—what goes down—it's all better with beautiful women. At least it's better for me."

The men all chuckled.

The woman's eyes opened on the post. Her head rolled back and forth. She blinked. She screamed.

—⚡—

The young man turned around and Carina was left with nothing to say or do in recourse.

"We're going back. We're not going to find anything out here."

The Doctor muttered something under his breath.

Carina stopped. "There's something out here though, someone screamed." She was whispering, but her words cut. "Don't you care that someone could be hurt?"

"Darling, they're probably back already. If you're concerned let's call the police."

She bit into her lip. "Alright, fine."

Behind her, she heard the sound of laughing men. Her cheeks burned.

"See?" said the young man. "Nothing wrong at all."

—⚡—

An icy breeze blew through the corn and the lot of them froze. The woman was still coming to, and she had just realized she was naked. She looked down at her body and confusion crossed her face.

"What's going on?" she asked. She said it like she was trying to play it cool, as if this wasn't a big deal, as if she didn't want to hurt anyone's feelings by being offended.

"Is this a joke?" she asked weakly.

The men stood back, their eyes to the earth.

"Wilbur? What's happening?" Fear cut her voice. "Why am I tied up? What did you do to me?"

"You don't have to answer, Wil."

"It's easier this way."

"Keep your eyes down and everything else will be taken care of." They had to hold his shoulders but he did as he was told.

"This is hard," he said.

"What's wrong? What's wrong? What's wrong?" she jabbered. Her words were sharp and jittery. Her eyes were wide and the whites of them glowed in the moonlight. She began to cry. Steve didn't think she was drunk anymore. Adrenaline was racing through her. She struggled against the ropes that tied her down. Camcorder resumed filming, as if this were the good part—the part he'd come to see.

Then: footsteps.

Heavy, confident footsteps. Dead corn crunched.

There were lots of them, maybe eight of them hidden in the cornfield.

Steve Calico put his hand in his mouth and bit down.

He felt them before he saw them.

One of them passed by, a mere inches from his face. Its soiled denim overalls brushed against his cheek and he bit down on his hand until blood dribbled down to the tips of his fingers, falling to the earth and mixing with the soil.

Oh shit.

Stalks swayed in the glow. And as they parted, he could see the one coming out from across the small clearing. It was the first one the woman saw too.

Six feet tall, adorned in ragged hand-me-downs. Straw poked out in spikes where skin should be. Its face was a mask—a face made of bound wheat with two dark holes of infinite black where eyes should be. As it appeared from the shadows, into the light, more followed.

The woman could not scream. She could not fathom what she was seeing. Her mouth gaped, she tried to force a noise out and Steve Calico thought about doing something, anything, but instead he just kept biting his knuckle and wishing desperately for this all to end. *God please make it stop, please stop and tell her it's a joke and we can all go home.*

The scarecrow pulled a scythe from his back, releasing it from the long leather strap holding it to his body. And as each of them appeared, approaching the woman, they each readied their weapon.

Wilbur cried, sobbed. He averted his eyes.

Scarecrows. They're walking scarecrows.

That was when Steve Calico couldn't do it anymore.

He stood up. His feet sank into the earth below him.

The blades slashed through the air. They whistled as they traveled.

Jesus.

The woman couldn't do anything, she moved impotently beneath her restraints.

The first blade caught her in the midsection—in one side and out the other. Its owner pulled on the long crescent and the woman let out a choking groan as it lifted her flesh. Before she could scream, another scythe stabbed deep into her shoulder blade. It entered and stood proudly from her like a headstone. Blood rolled out of the wound and this time, Steve was sure she would scream—

But there was another blade. Another hateful swing.

Blood bubbled from her neck and her eyes were those of an animal. She was trying to talk, but the words kept geysering from her throat.

The scarecrows stood silent, monoliths in the corn.

Blood continued to pour from her wounds. Her body was going into shock. She was pale and speaking softly the language of absolute and eternal nonsense.

Why aren't I running?

Oh God. He hadn't moved a muscle.

Steve Calico felt as frozen and helpless as the girl and he very much wanted to go.

Okay, I'm going to move now. Away from the dying girl, away from the straw-men, away from the crying lover, away from the—

The first scarecrow, who had swung his scythe horizontal through the woman's stomach, pulled it free with one good yank. The flesh between its entry and exit points gave easily. There was a wet sound, a slushing noise, and the woman's babbling ended with her guts unraveling into the earth. When her body went limp, Steve Calico ran.

Carina sat on the porch steps. They'd come back to red and blue lights.

"If something happened here, we'll know about it. That's for goddamned sure."

The officer told her to sit down, to relax. He walked across the lawn to the doctor and the young man. Carina saw them laughing together.

The air smelled of autumn and something else.

Tears welled in her eyes.

She could taste it on her lips as the officers went into the corn. She could taste it on the vowels of their party guests. She could see it rimming the moon.

It was old and wise and resolute and she could taste it.

She knew it in her bones.

Emily was dead and she could taste the blood.

AND SO IT GOES, WE ARE FED.

WHEN THE COLD COMES, WE KNOW IT'S OUR TURN AT THE TROUGH, AND WE GIVE BACK WHAT WE CAN. WE GIVE BACK FOOD WE CANNOT EAT, MONEY WE CANNOT SPEND, PROSPERITY WE DO NOT KNOW.

WE HAVE TOILED IN THIS LAND, FOREVER. AND SO TOO DOES IT BLEED WELL.

BUT, SOMETHING IN US CHANGES, BECOMES ANIMAL, WHEN WE SEE YOU RUN.

WHEN YOU RUN, THEY SAY: "STOP HIM!"

SO, WE MUST.

WE MOVE TOGETHER LIKE THE BLACK BIRDS. WE DO NOT FEEL AT HOME IN OUR BODIES AND WE LIKELY NEVER WILL, WE ITCH WITHIN THEIR PROPORTIONS BUT ALAS WE ARE DISCIPLINED— WE MOVE AS ONE. MAYBE YOU COULD LEARN FROM US.

You run hard, throwing yourself into the dirt, as if getting closer to the earth will save you. It will not.

The earth has always been ours.

It tells us secrets you cannot fathom.

We don't get you at first. Our blades stab short. Your legs work hard to propel you. You scramble across the dirt like a scared rat. You're so used to the bones and meat that are your vessel. Is it like the earth is to us? The trees? The cawing of birds? The wetness of blood? To know something so wholly—even a body—is to love it. You must love it, every hair and scrunching muscle. Every bead of sweat; every hot breath panting from your lips. If you didn't love it, why would you work so hard to protect it?

And it takes us only one drop of your vessel's nectar to realize that the greatest lie ever told was scarcity.

Have we ever been so well fed?

You are abundant.

And we are hungry.

We hook you by the heel and you scream with a mouthful of earth. You kick with your good leg as we pull you between the rows, so we can look at you—clearly, for the first time.

You twist around like a worm on a hook and we see your terror. We are all around you. We will swallow you.

You keep squirming, each blade laying

CLAIM TO YOUR FLESH. WE ARE THE WORLD'S OLDEST WORKERS AND WE ARE WORKING NOW. WE ARE DISMANTLING WHAT THIS EARTH HAS GROWN UNDER OUR WATCH.

AND YOU TASTE GOOD.

AND YOU ARE PLENTIFUL.

AND WE REALIZE, HERE IN THE SILVER LIGHT, AS THE COLD WIND LAPS AT YOUR EXPOSED WOUNDS—WE REALIZE THAT WE DO NOT NEED TO BE FED.

WE CAN FEED OURSELVES.

CHAPTER TWELVE

T HEY FOUND THE body within an hour.

A woman.

At first it was just a woman. She wasn't Emily until the morning.

Carina didn't sleep. The party ended when the ambulance came and she spent the rest of the night crying.

Wilbur was crying too, when he came out. And the others, they were shaken, but they patted him on the back and said that these sorts of things just happen.

She tried asking him what happened. When he was alone, while the others were talking to the police. He looked at her with the reddest eyes and said, "We lost her. She ran off."

And that was that.

Slowly, details emerged.

Emily had tripped, fallen, and hit her head on a rock. That's what one officer told her the next day when she came to collect more evidence.

"It was dark, she'd been drinking. It happens."

Carina swallowed and nodded. "Of course."

But I saw the body. I saw the red seeping through the sheet they covered her with. I saw pieces of her dangling out.

But none of that mattered.

Emily Mueller hit her head and died quickly on impact.

And Carina felt an ache in her soul, a lavish, expensive pain that resonated through her every waking minute. She could not speak without crying. She could not eat without crying. The very air she breathed formed lumps in her throat. Sadness was a cancer that feasted on her from the inside out and outside in.

Larry Dell called her the following evening. She was so delirious with grief she barely understood what he was saying. She played her part.

His voice was solemn, honeyed. He said, "I've covered your shifts for the rest of the week. I know this must be hard for you."

Carina choked. "Thank you," she said. But when she tried to say anything else, nothing came out.

"Wilbur is having a rough time of it, him and the girl. The funeral's on Sunday, I'm supposed to tell you."

"How's Hazel doing?"

"She's been better."

"Of course. I feel so awful for her."

"We all do. It's not easy for a child."

They spoke for only a moment more, when Larry Dell excused himself, as there was work to be done at the store.

When the call ended she was left with her grief.

The whole of Greentree seemed to be in some ritualistic contortion over the death of Emily Mueller. She was well-liked, Carina decided—at least according to the size of her funeral. There were several hundred people in attendance, many of them people she had seen around town—bankers, businessman, managers, real estate agents—they all gathered to offer their sympathies in unison, each with a pat on the back for Wilbur Mueller and a stooping bend to Hazel, to tell her that they did indeed know how hard it was, how hard it was going to be for a while.

There was no church in Greentree, Carina learned; only a crematorium. To lay Carina to rest, they traveled out of town, right on the other side of the city limits. It was white and had a bell and a steeple. It looked like it were a cutout of a children's book, as if it were the archetypical small town American church—out in the middle of nowhere, as if not to taint Greentree with death. She drove there in silence, a heaviness in her stomach. She did not want to have to say goodbye. As she went beyond the pines, her heart broke again and again.

At the funeral, she found Hazel first.

She wore a black shirt and black jeans and her hair was dyed black and really, she assumed that her father had given up the fight the morning of the funeral, with good reason. She stared at her shoes and sat in a corner, hidden from their guest's attention.

"How are you doing?" asked Carina. "I've been worried about you."

The girl jumped, covering her mouth as she yelped. "I didn't see you there."

"Sorry, you were just all alone. I wanted to see how you were doing."

Her shoulders raised in a half-hearted shrug. "I'm fucking sad, what do you think?"

Carina sat down behind her. The sermon was over and the rest of them were commingling between the pews, approaching the coffin and laying flowers. *A closed casket.*

"I'm sad too."

Hazel sniffed."You knew my Mom for a long time, huh?"

"Yeah."

"Was she always so fucking boring?" Her words choked on their way out.

Carina laughed. "No, but I never thought she was boring to begin with. I thought she had it all figured out."

"Yeah, but it doesn't matter now, does it?"

"I want to believe that it matters."

She scoffed. "Of course you do." They were quiet for a moment and then Hazel said, "When are you going back to work?" She fidgeted with her fingers. "It's worse there without you."

"You've been working?"

She nodded. "I can't stand being home with *him*." She motioned to her father, tangled in his peers' pity. "It's awkward. He doesn't know what he's doing."

Carina considered this. "I don't think any of us know what we're doing when it comes to *this*."

Hazel looked up to her with puffy red eyes and said, "I just miss my Mom."

Carina fell to her, wrapping her in her arms. She cooed in Hazel's ear as the girl cried into her shoulder. Her sobs were violent and they brought the same out in Carina. Soon, the two women were both crying and they were the only ones in the whole church with tears in their eyes.

✦

The Mueller's home was now filled with casseroles and people. Carina came at Hazel's request, unsure if she were truly welcomed. Still, when she saw him for the first time face to face, Wilbur patted her on the back. They were alone in the kitchen.

"I just don't know what happened," he said matter-of-factly.

"We went out to look for you, you know."

He turned his back to wash a plate in the sink.

"We heard a scream," said Carina.

Wilbur sighed.

"What happened out there?"

"She was drunk. She tripped. She fell." He muttered. "Must've been a sharp rock, or something."

"Aren't the rocks tilled out, before the corn is planted?"

Wilbur washed his dish and turned to her. He shook his head. "Please, Carina—nobody plants that corn."

CHAPTER THIRTEEN

IT WAS ONE full week after Emily died that life began to find its routine. Greentree, the sleepy town that it was, swept away its grief as if it were dirt on the linoleum. Carina, waking up in the early morning, with her coffee and sun rise, felt her sorrow was out of place. She stuck out like a sore thumb and felt an urge to conform, to heal. So, in a relatively short amount of time, she learned to smile again. People wanted her to smile. She realized there was some universal law at work in Greentree and she was finding she must abide by it. The problem was that people, in general, did not like sadness. True, sometimes it was cathartic, and that was what they enjoyed—a brief explosion, an outburst, an orgasm—but when it lingered, when it began to swallow life, it became useless, performative. When sadness became too overbearing, people responded with platitudes—a dozen rotating sayings that started with "At least it's not . . . "

Carina went back to work and faced Hazel again, who seemed to have learned the same lesson. She was bored, angsty, with only brief outbursts of agony, now using what she called "the dead mom card" to get out of family dinners, late shifts, or questions she didn't want to answer.

But when Hazel went back to school, no longer able to flex her tragedy, Carina found herself with Jessica. Indomitable, soon-to-graduate, and particular.

"How are you guys rotating the displays?"

"I was never told to do that."

"Carina, honey," she said with oblivious condescension. "We need to keep the displays fresh. Put some old favorites up there!"

"Okay," said Carina.

"And don't put up anything rated R."

"Alright."

"And nothing that's not uplifting."

"Did you have something in mind?"

"No, just choose movies you think will represent the store well."

"Got it," she said.

Jessica managed under a microscope. She adjusted barcodes on DVD cases to be perfectly symmetrical. She hovered over other clerks to be sure they used the correct syntax when describing damage in their computer system. Her eyes were made to find fault and they did so with a bouncy enthusiasm that made Carina dread pulling into the Stardust.

Luckily for Carina though, the Stardust was busier than ever.

"Something's in the air," said Jessica, shrugging theatrically. All of her movements were those of a performer.

Carina heard the rustling of the beaded curtain. She cocked her head, narrowed her eyes. "Don't you think its strange how many of our customers are going to the Adults section now?" Carina asked it as an afterthought. A curiosity. She'd noticed a bump of rentals, a lot of men and women disappearing behind those beaded curtains with a blank DVD in a clear jewel case held to their chest.

But Jessica didn't think it strange at all, apparently. She only said, "I don't concern myself with customer buying habits. The Stardust does not share information on personal rentals."

"Okay," said Carina, shrugging, shrinking. "Understood."

⬩

It was a late October evening when she got home from work. Three weeks after Emily's death. She'd stopped jogging. She had not healed, but she was functional. She came back to the old farmhouse and drank in its beauty.

There was a note on her door.

Folded in half, poor handwriting facing outward—it read simply: *Carina.*

She read in on the front porch, the sunset behind her.

"Because of recent events . . ."

" . . . financial burden . . ."

" . . . monthly lease . . ."

"Sign and return . . ."

"Sincerely, Wilbur Mueller."

She folded the letter up and put it in the pocket of her jeans, where even if she maintained that it was fair and fine, it still burned.

Out in the field, below the wall of pines, amongst the corn where old souls roamed—a hunger deepened.

Their bodies twitched as the sun set, as they always did, as if they were itching to embody their shells with every bit of darkness that came. As the sun further dimmed, they moved as if by a phantom wind. And when the night finally fell, they were no longer frozen vessels.

CHAPTER FOURTEEN

CRACKLING STRAW. *The snaps and crunches of dried plant matter. Corn stalks lashed against her face, hundreds of switches with leaves like a cat's tongue.*

She ran.

Loping footsteps behind her. Long, uneven strides. It sounded like the thing was hurt, or incomplete in some manner. That it could not run. And yet it was. Because of Carina. Because it wanted to chase her. Because no matter how much it hurt, it would endure the pain if only to catch her in its grasp. The thought sickened her. Why does it want me? Why does it care? Why can't I just live in peace? These questions were all born with a tremor in her throat.

It was dark and there was nothing but an endless eternity of corn. And she kept running, and the thing she-heard-but-could-not-see kept chasing her.

I need to get out of here, she thought. She stopped for a moment, sweat dewing her brow. She turned in a circle, to try to find some way out. There was nothing. Only a devouring blackness and a sense of impending doom.

Maybe if I close my eyes, I can disappear, she thought.

She tried. The blackness of the field was replaced with the blackness of her eyelids. The footsteps continued.

No no no no. Panic spiked within her chest. Her heart was mid-tantrum, screaming. She opened her eyes.

She said a short prayer to honor small victories. The moon. It was so bright. How did she miss it before?

The corn gleamed silver in the moonlight.

But the sound was closer. That horrible rustling was only steps away. Chills erupted all over her, as if her body was trying its best to reject its sensory inputs. Shutting down, purging data. Refusing the world around it.

And then the corn parted. Not behind her, like she was expecting. Right in front of her. An inch from her face.

Carina jumped back, grasping at her heart, shrieking.

Emily's face emerged from the corn. Her eyes were milky, her skin was drained of blood. The muscles under her skin were rock hard. Death was not peaceful, apparently, it was tense. Her jaw was clenched. Her teeth were bared. And her hands stretched out in front of her like bony talons.

"I'm sorry," said Carina. "I'm sorry!"

But Emily couldn't hear her. Or perhaps didn't care. Because she continued forward. Carina couldn't run anymore. Her body had failed her. She closed her eyes and waited, bracing for the ice cold touch of death—intimately aware that it would be a feeling her body could not purge.

Carina woke up.

There was no corn. Just a room. Just an inky sky bleeding drops of sunlight.

Just a dream.

But while the imagery of her dream drifted away, the anxiety didn't.

She almost just closed her eyes, went back to sleep. She was used to that, because she was used to being wrong. She was used to questioning her own senses.

Her eyes wide in the dark—she was used to that too.

But now, it was different.

Her eyes had adjusted. Her heart continued to pound.

There was no mistaking it this time—a tall black shape loomed within the rectangle of her doorframe

"Who is it?"

No answer. She got out of bed. Her blood was hot and she panted out of panic. *Oh God, no. Oh God, I'm not ready.*

She was sure she would die.

She rushed over to turn on the lights. But even she knew this was useless. The shape had moved. It was walking away. She could hear its footsteps.

Haunted, she thought. The word came to her again and again. *I live in a haunted house.*

With the light from her room bleeding into the hallway, she stepped out. She listened. They were not just one set of footsteps, there were many.

She heard them creaking and shuffling all around her, all of them just out of her vision.

"Who's here?" she shouted.

And no one answered.

It took her thirty minutes to descend the stairs. Each step felt monumental in itself. She jumped at every creek as the house settled. But by the time she got to the main floor, there was no sound at all.

Her heart was beating in her head. An unceasing *whump-whump-whump*. For a moment, she was sure she was having a heart attack. She was dizzy. She held onto the banister for balance. It passed. She was alone.

The house was empty.

The clock said it was 4 am. *Too early.*

Her tense body relaxed. She walked down the stairs tentatively. The house was quiet. She made herself coffee and sat on the porch. She held a flashlight in her hands and she shined it on the corn every time she thought she heard something. She did this often.

And when the sun came up, her heart beat hard in her chest again.

She dropped her coffee. It splashed against her legs but she couldn't be bothered by that. She stood from her chair and stepped through the puddle, feeling the heat between her toes. She went to the wooden railing, mouth agape.

Across the field of corn that stretched to the tall black pines, were the dozens of scarecrows all atop their posts, their straw and burlap faces staring out with coal eyes. She realized, in a breathless moment, that they were staring at her.

As the sun came up, glinting over the horizon, so too did their blades. No longer rusted, nicked, and dull, but sharp—very, very sharp.

CHAPTER FIFTEEN

SATURDAYS WERE THE best days for Carina, because she knew she would see Hazel. She didn't quite understand why or how Hazel had become her best friend, but she sometimes saw Emily in her, the Emily she knew in college. The old Emily was a force of nature—she had not yet settled for anything and seemed unprepared for anything but excellence. It was refreshing, for someone as demure as Carina, to see someone *demand*. Carina was not in the business of demanding. But Emily was and so was Hazel, and while they wanted different things, they were both sure they could get them.

"What's up, Cari?"

"How are you?"

"My mom's dead. Stop using that *how are you* voice with me. You know I'm fucking sad." She didn't say it like she was sad though. "How are you doing?"

"Probably about the same as you."

"Well, bam—you got your answer."

"Hey, Hazel, I wanted to ask you a question."

"Shoot."

"Do you know anything about the house I'm staying in?"

"Oh, you mean the Emily Mueller Memorial Bed and Breakfast?"

"That's the one."

Hazel rolled her eyes. "Not much to know. Just some basic Greentree history. They teach it in schools around here."

"As they should. So what do you know?"

"That it's basically an antique, a roadside attraction. One of the founders of Greentree used to live there, some sort of magnate."

"A magnet?"

"Like a big-business dude."

"Oh, gotcha."

"I can't remember the name but he basically built the town, sometime at the turn of the century." She narrowed her eyes. "*Your* turn of the century, not mine."

"Of course," said Carina, stifling a smile. "Anything else to this tale?"

"Nope. Old dude died, left the house in disrepair. Was uninhabited for a long time, but Dad liked it and bought it."

"If it's such a town treasure why did no one keep it going?"

Hazel shrugged. She reached out to a stack of DVDs, rolling her fingers down the spines. "I think it was a piece of shit. Like, huge project. Lot of work needed to done."

"But the owner was loaded?"

"He was kind of a slob though too. Like that airplane guy."

"Howard Hughes. He made movies too, you know."

"I just know Leo played him. Larry *loves* Leo. *Wolf of Wall Street* obsessed, you know?"

"So, he was mentally ill?"

"Maybe. Or just gross. Either way."

Carina sighed. She wasn't sure how much she wanted to tell Hazel. "I've been having bad dreams."

"Me too."

"I don't think we're having the same kind of dreams. I keep feeling like I'm being watched. Or there's someone in the house."

"Maybe there is."

"Don't say that."

"Don't bitch if you don't want a solution."

"What do you think I should do then?"

"I think you should investigate the situation."

"And how would I do that?"

"God, you're such a fucking nerd sometimes, you know that? Haven't you seen *Paranormal Activity*? You work at a video store, right? Set up some cameras and film the house while you sleep."

Carina smiled. "But I don't have any cameras."

"Borrow one from Larry. He's got a ton. He films just about everything. Has a little videography business on the side."

"Wow, another magnate."

"Jesus, Larry has like five businesses. He's fucking loaded. He's a creep."

"Your Mom liked him."

"My Mom liked everyone. She needed to like everyone so that they'd like her back. That's how she was." Hazel blinked. She cleared her throat. "My Dad wanted me to invite you over for dinner tonight, by the way."

"Sure," said Carina, hiding her discomfort. She felt like Wilbur had been trying to avoid her since the wake. "I'd love to."

"Of course you would—that's why you were friends with my Mom."

The Greentree Public Library was a small building, a two-story rectangle of red brick with large windows. On the front door, there were fliers posted, and inside there was a children's section fitted with toys and books and signs pleading for silence. Watching over the children's section at the front desk was a single bespectacled man. A sign with arrows pointed around the library. Fiction over here. Computers over here. Non-fiction over here. Archives down there.

Carina pushed through the door and the old man nodded at her serenely. "New around here?"

"I've been here for almost two months."

"That's new, for sure. Do you have a card?"

"No, not yet."

"Well, shit. We better get you a card, then." He happily took her information, ooh-ing and ah-ing at where she came from, who she was, where she was staying.

"Old house, out there."

"Do you know about it?"

"No more than anyone else, but we have some books on it, of course."

"That's just what I was looking for."

"Brushing up on local history?"

"That's right. I figured if I'm going to live here . . . "

She stopped. On the desk was a small container filled with bookmarks. There was a watercolor printed on it—a field of scarecrows and an old farmhouse. Above the painting it said Greentree Public Library, below it said: *Painting courtesy of Emily Mueller*. She swallowed and the old man reached a hand out to her.

"It's a shame about Emily. She was a good one. Nice woman. Talented, too."

"You knew her?" She knew she sounded stupid, but her voice cracked and the old man just nodded sadly.

"I did. Pretty well. She used to be here all the time. Sometimes she'd teach painting to the kids."

"I didn't know that."

He nodded to the stack of bookmarks. "You can take some, if you like. They're free. Something to remember your friend by."

She did as he suggested, sliding three bookmarks into the pocket of her coat. "Um," she found her words slowly. "I'm sorry. Do you have any old newspapers?"

"We got archives going for years. I can help you with whatever you need. I'm good for that. Always have been, always will be. Name's Ben, by the way, if you care."

She smiled. "Thank you, Ben."

"Here's your card. You're welcome, Carina."

The downstairs was covered in a film of dust. Even breathing, Carina felt its mustiness. Ben confirmed what she suspected. "Nobody ever really comes down here, nobody needs to," he said. "Anyone who lives here knows what they need to know and that's that."

At the Stardust, she'd made a short list while no one was around. "I'm looking for newspapers, obituaries from October of last year, and the year before."

Ben whistled. "We've got a detective here."

Carina raised an eyebrow. "Why do you say that?"

He smiled slightly, a smile that wasn't particularly happy or sad—only knowing. "There's always talk of a curse around here. Not really a curse though, more of sustained bad luck—that's what I'd call it. You're talking about the Autumn Autopsies, right?"

"A girl at my work said the kids talk about people dying every October."

He opened a filing cabinet, his fingers working spider-like through their contents. "We called it the Autumn Autopsies when I was a kid. Morbid name, but kids are sometimes morbid."

"Does it really happen every year?"

"What? People dying? Of course it does. But that doesn't mean a thing, really. People die every month, even in Greentree. We're not immune to man's mortality. What happens in October is bizarre—maybe it has to do with the season, ghosts and ghouls and what have you—something sweet in the wind—everything's dying in Fall, why not us? But these deaths aren't like regular deaths. They're usually inexplicable, strange. Rumors always circle about these sorts of things though. There's no escaping those rumors."

Carina nodded. "I see."

"You'll wanna be in front of the microfiche for this. But I can load it up for you. Let me know if you need anything else."

"Thank you."

Ben left her in silence, in the basement of the old library. The building reminded her of the house, how it creaked in the night, how it settled.

She went to the year prior and looked at newspaper clippings. It took her a minute to find it. But there it was: *Kayla Collins Found Dead in Woods—Wild Animals Suspected.*

Another year back.

Local Woman Dies in Thresher Accident.

Susanna Delmert Passes Away in Hit and Run.

They went back years, decades at least. Carina found every one of them nestled somewhere in the local paper, between late September and Halloween. Each of them were banal, painfully usual—and almost every single one of them died on the outskirts of town.

And they were all women.

This proves nothing.

And it didn't. She didn't know anything besides that some people had died. She flipped forward into time.

Woman, Intoxicated, Suffers Life-Ending Trip-and-Fall Accident.

That was Emily, right there—a whole life diluted to a headline. Where she was drunk, clumsy, and dead.

She went up the stairs, feeling defeated. *Yes, people die here. But, so? People die everywhere.*

"Find what you were looking for?" Ben watched her from behind his glasses, perched perfectly on the tip of his nose.

"I guess. I wasn't sure what I was looking for."

He smiled. "It's part of my job to help with that too." He lifted a book from the table. "I went ahead and found this for you. A little Greentree history. Maybe it can be of use."

She picked the book up: *An Oral History of Greentree, Oregon* by Sabrina Waterbrook.

"Thank you," she said.

And Ben just laughed. "Oh God, don't thank me. I don't want to be thanked for this."

Chapter Sixteen

T HE MUELLER FAMILY home was dark. Hazel tried to explain it when she let Carina in. "A couple light bulbs went out. Dad's been working a lot, so . . . " Her words trailed off and Carina just nodded. She'd never seen Hazel like this. She was acting like a host, like her mother would have.

Wilbur walked into the room. He seemed taller than the last time she saw him. He towered over her and Hazel like a cracking obelisk. "Carina, hello," he said. His lips spread in a mechanical smile. "I'm so happy you were able to join us tonight."

"No problem at all." Her voice squeaked when she said it.

"How's work?"

"Good, fine. The same."

He nodded slowly. "Old Larry not running you too ragged?"

"No, I barely see him."

"Ah yeah, that Larry—always busy."

There was silence for a moment. "Food will be here soon. I ordered out. Make yourself at home."

"Okay."

In the living room, she and Hazel talked while Wilbur stood outside, apparently waiting for pizza to show up. They spoke only in formalities, because the house was so oppressive they didn't know what else they could say. Everything felt taboo. Between sentences, silence hung like an iron chain around their necks. When a cheese pizza arrived, they politely ate while Wilbur watched them from across the table.

"Did you get my letter?" he asked.

"Yes," said Carina. "I did."

"Good. I know it's unexpected, but—"

"No explanation is needed. It's your property, you have the right to do what you want with it."

"Of course. It shouldn't just be there, you know?"

"I'm happy to pay rent while I'm here."

"Emily was never good at that sort of thing. She always wanted to hand out freebies. She always wanted everyone to like her."

She couldn't look at him. "Emily was a good person."

"She was," he said simply.

She felt Hazel's hand on her knee. Pleading for her to be careful; *there be monsters ahead.*

He shook his head. "I loved Em."

Carina stole a glance at Hazel. The girl's eyes were dry, bored, downcast.

"We're buying more property," he said. "My business is better than ever." Tears formed in his eyes and he cleared his throat. "I'm going to be a millionaire." After the last word, he abruptly got up to leave the table, practically running from the kitchen.

Hazel leaned over to her and whispered. "Please, get me out of here."

Carina stood up from the table and followed Wilbur's clunking footsteps.

The bathroom door was closed, but she could hear his muffled sobs through the door.

"Hey, Wil?"

There was a long pause. "Just a moment," said the strained voice. "I just need a moment."

"I had an idea."

"What?"

"How would you feel if I took Hazel to the B & B for a couple of days? It could give you some time to work or whatever."

She heard him breathing through the door. "Yeah, okay. Fine," he said. "Take her."

She waited for him to say anything else, but the door stayed shut and he made no signs of turning the lock.

"Okay then," she said. "I'll take her over tonight, maybe for the weekend."

"Sure." The word was a dead note, empty.

"Dinner was lovely, Wilbur. She'll be safe."

Hazel waited at the dinner table, a slice of pizza in her mouth. "Well?"

"You can stay over at the farmhouse through the weekend." She stopped, to see if Wilbur's sobs could be heard from the dining room. Silence. "Maybe longer," she said. "I don't know."

Hazel sighed. "Cool."

"Let's go. Now."

Hazel packed quickly while Carina waited by the door, toe tapping against her will. *Why am I so nervous? I've got nothing to be scared of, do I? He's just struggling.*

It wouldn't be so unbelievable for a bereaved husband to throw himself into his work for the sake of his own sanity, to sweep his grief under the rug and focus instead on the betterment of his family—but there was something so unhinged, painful about Wilbur's actions, something so—

Guilty.

She swallowed.

"Hazel? Are you almost ready?"

"Yes, yes—coming."

⎯⎯✦⎯⎯

"We'll need cameras, of course," said Hazel.

"Cameras?"

"That's why I'm staying, right? I'm helping with the ghosts?"

"I thought you needed time away from your father."

"That too," she said. "But we could kill two birds with one stone, couldn't we? See what's going on with that house?"

Carina shrugged, her hands on the wheel. "I suppose we could. What harm could it do?"

"Exactly."

She thought of telling Hazel that she went to the library after work, but didn't. Hazel didn't seem scared anymore; she was preoccupied, excited.

Hazel ran up to the farmhouse door and rang the doorbell playfully and Carina came behind her, slower, already worried that this was the sort of mistake she'd regret. She now felt the weight of Hazel's backpack; the strap was pulling down on her shoulder and she leaned to one side as she lugged it.

Inside, she immediately went to the couch. Hazel made herself at home.

"Mom really liked this place," she said, unzipping her backpack. "I think that's why she let you live here."

94

"She did a great job with it."

"Of course she did. She's Mom—she did a great job at everything she wanted to do."

Hazel upended the backpack and emptied its contents on the couch. Sleek black electronics fell out onto the couch cushions with a mess of wires. "We'll have to get them back to the Stardust before Larry flips."

Cameras.

Carina's mouth made an 'o.' "You stole those?"

Hazel shook her head. "You know what I'm going to say already, so why don't you say it for me?"

Carina found herself mouthing the words, against her own will. "You'd say: 'No, I borrowed them.'"

"Right. Larry won't miss them for an evening. If he does—well, fuck him."

"I don't know, Hazel . . . This doesn't seem right."

"It'll be fine. And this way, we can know for sure what's going on here."

Carina pursed her lips. "Tell me," she said. "Why do you think anything is going on at all?"

"You said you've been hearing things."

"Sure, but people hear things all the time, right?"

"Yes, of course. But those people aren't you. Have you looked at yourself lately, Cari? Do you even know who you are?"

Carina threw her arms out, like: *what am I supposed to look like?*

"You're the type of woman who would walk with a rock in her shoe rather than take it off and take it out. You're a coper. You don't fix things, it's not your nature. Your nature is resilience, but not in the good way. In the shitty way. You're a martyr and you're good at it. My mother said you're the type to suffer in silence for an invisible audience—so, for you to have a problem and come to someone with it? To admit something is wrong in the first place? Well, that's a big fucking problem."

Hazel picked up a camcorder and put her eye to its viewfinder. She aimed it at Carina, who wilted in front of its lens. "Plus, there's all the stories."

Stories. "You're talking about the Autumn Autopsies," Carina said.

Hazel nodded. "Never thought Mom would be one of them. Name feels gross to say now." Sorrow formed a brief shadow across her face, making her look much older than her sixteen years. But, with a sudden and sharp inhale of breath, she banished it to some deep and secret part of her—hidden deep from where Carina could see. "Everything bad happens out here," she said. "Everyone dies out here. *Everyone.*"

Carina saw herself in the black lens of the camera, her face a tan mask. Her heart stuttered and she felt an old, familiar sense of dread pool in her stomach, a lead weight that sank as she saw the glint in the girl's eye. *Everyone dies out here. Everyone.*

Chapter Seventeen

We have always allowed the mortals their own brick fields and they have allowed us our own. They gave us shape and we gave them life. It is true that we loved them for this. It is our shapes that protect us. They did not make us but they did fashion our bodies into their image. And for that, we will always feel some kinship to those who rule us.

But sons kill their fathers; mothers drown their daughters—history is brimming with families slain by their kin.

It is blood that brings prosperity and we are the drawers of blood. And yet, we are not the beneficiaries of blood, only of shape.

We move swiftly, climbing from our posts as the sun dips below the horizon and the sky becomes an inky indigo. The corn provides our shadows, but we do not need to hide. Their shape rests at night. It's as if the earth demands that feet tread across it. When one sleeps, the other rises. When they dream, we watch. Memories, fantasies, the constant tug of something in

THEIR GUTS THAT MAKES THEM WANT. SOME PRIMAL DESIRE—A HUNGER—THAT IS A PALE SHADOW TO OUR OWN. YES, WE SEE IT ALL.

WE FOLLOW THOSE DREAMS, WE DRAG OUR SCYTHES ACROSS THEM TO SHARPEN OUR BLADES. WE FOLLOW THEM FROM STREET TO STREET. WE PEER INTO WINDOWS AND BREATHE THEM INTO OUR BURLAP LUNGS.

AN OLD WOMAN. SHE TOILS IN HER SHOP MOST OF THE DAY. AT NIGHT SHE DOES THE SAME. YES, SHE HAS DREAMS.

WE WATCH HER FROM HER WINDOWS. SHE TALKS TO HERSELF. WE WATCH. OUR BLADES UNSHEATHE.

SHE CUPS HER EAR. SHE PAUSES. A BRANCH SNAPPING, THE RUSTLING OF COTTON. SHE LOOKS HURRIEDLY TO THE WINDOW, HER JAW OPENING AS IF IT WERE UNHINGED—BECAUSE SHE SEES SOMETHING. A SHAPE.

<hr>

The cameras were set up quickly and Carina tried her best to follow Hazel's explanations. The cameras were connected to the internet, which was connected to her phone, and somehow . . .

Carina didn't understand it, not really. But she saw Hazel on her phone, flipping through camera angles like it was second nature. The living room, the stairs, outside of Carina's room, inside of Carina's room.

"You're gonna watch me sleep?"

"Yep."

"What if I sleep nude?"

"Please don't."

Carina laughed. "What do we do now?"

"We're going to do what we normally do—or should I say, what you normally do."

Carina thought. She was almost embarrassed. "I usually just read, maybe have some coffee."

Hazel shook her head. "Alright, old lady—then, get to it."

Despite her jab, for the rest of the night, Hazel did the same. She did not mention her father or mother and maintained a jovial attitude, silently reading while sipping tea. She devoured horror paperbacks with long titles and lurid covers. She retired to the room beside Carina's.

Carina tried not to look out there, for fear of what she might see. There were other things to think about. Panic could be ignored, for now. Fear could be vanquished.

Sometimes, she imagined Steve Calico waiting, his vicious smile and silver tongue waiting patiently for the police. She often had to start talking when that happened, to force new images in her head.

But *An Oral History of Greentree* was more than sufficiently interesting. She read to herself while the wind rustled outside, and she saw Greentree in all its ancient glory—a farming community where turn of the century industrialists set down roots for their retirement.

—✦—

SHE KEEPS CALLING FOR HER SON.

"LARRY. LARRY. LARRY. WHERE ARE YOU, LARRY? PLEASE!"

WE ARE IN HER HOME. SHE TRIES TO RUN BUT HER BODY FAILS HER. SHE FALLS AND WE HEAR THE CRACK OF HER BRITTLE BONES AS SHE HITS THE FLOOR.

SHE IS AN ANIMAL, DOOMED TO DIE.

OUR BLADES PROD HER PAPERY FLESH. OUR METAL FINGERS TEAR AT HER CLOTHES. SHE JERKS BACK AND FORTH, HER BACK TO THE FLOOR.

SHE LIVED A LONG LIFE.

WE DELIVER UNTO HER FOUR STROKES OF RECLAMATION.

FIRST: TO HER PALE AND DISTENDED STOMACH—A GRAZING GASH THAT BLOSSOMS WITH DARK RED BLOOD. IT SPILLS OUT IN STRANDS DOWN HER SIDE AND ONTO THE FLOOR.

HER HANDS EXPLORE THIS NEW CAVERN. HER EYES WIDEN WITH DISBELIEF. PANIC SPUTTERS FROM HER LIPS.

THE BLOOD SOAKS THROUGH THE WOOD, SEEPS THROUGH THE FLOORBOARDS, DRIPS TO THE EARTH AND WE CAN TASTE IT.

SECOND: A SWIFT SLASH THAT SHE DOESN'T FEEL AS IT HAPPENS. THE BLADE GOES IN ONE SIDE OF HER HEAD AND OUT THE OTHER. IT IS A SHALLOW SWING, THE METAL EDGE OF THE BLADE BISECTING HER EYES. WITH A SHORT, SHARP SNAP, THE EYES VOMIT BLOOD AND PINK JELLY. SHE DOES NOT SEE THE THIRD AND FOURTH STRIKES, BUT SHE FEELS THEM. THEY LIFT HER UP OFF THE GROUND, FIT AROUND HER THROAT LIKE AN ELEGANT NECKLACE.

SHE STOPS MOVING, EVENTUALLY. ONLY SHALLOW BREATHS BETRAY ANY SEMBLANCE OF LIFE LEFT IN HER. SHE KNEW SHE WOULD BE RETURNED TO THE EARTH. HER LUNGS STILL WHEN WE, AS A COLLECTIVE, END HER LIFE. SHE IS IN PIECES WHEN WE FINISH.

———

Waterbrook—*An Oral History of Greentree, Oregon*— Page 8

The early days of Greentree were intimately intertwined with Cameron Green—the town's namesake, first mayor, greatest advocate, and perhaps its richest inhabitant in history.

Green was an industrialist interested in revolutionizing the American farmers' life with new technology. While farming had continued to innovate in the years prior, especially as the country moved west and more food was needed to feed those who could afford, Green was more obsessed with famine than equipment. He famously said, "There will always be newer and better machines, but even these will need to be used with good sense."

This good sense was the driving force behind his empire. But unlike his quote suggests, which paints him as a mere almanac salesman, Green did much of what his contemporaries did when it came to selling. He only did it better. He sold the first tractors to wealthy farmers in the mid-1890s, but his Good Sense came as a guarantee. What Cameron Green did to differentiate himself from his competitors was to not only sell tractors, but to sell consultants. These consultants, available for free with the purchase of a tractor, would come to a farmer's property and test soil, map the sun, take temperatures, and then provide recommendations for the next planting season. Green was not selling farm equipment, he was selling expertise. And it worked.

But, it was not until the turn of the century that Green came to Oregon. It was 1902 and it was widely believed, at least amongst the more rumor-friendly papers of the time, that the agriculture magnate had died, but truth can be stranger than fiction. His company had been given new leadership, and Green was nowhere to be found. But, he was certainly not dead.

Around this time, Green had a change of heart and fell in with a group of spiritualists. Little was known about this group, but they reportedly had members in such contemporary celebrities as Aleister Crowley and Oscar Wilde. They called themselves the Knights of Commerce and believed in a sort of proto-Objectivism, the likes of which would become popular in the writings of Ayn Rand years later. Their beliefs were both spiritual and capitalistic, merging free market theory with an interest in the supernatural. Little is known about this time in Green's life, only that when he came out from hiding, he had a fresh sense of vitality about him. Upon his public resurfacing, he announced he would be creating a new, wholly self-sustained township in the Oregon wilderness.

He went from city to city on the East coast, finding devout followers at each stop on his tours. Together, they would make the trek across the country. Newspapers at the time called this migration The New Oregon Trail and—

A creak.

Carina put the book down on her bed.

Her first instinct was to call out, but she was overwhelmed by the urge to listen.

Then, from the room next to hers: "Cari, did you hear that?"

She took a deep breath. "Yes," she said finally. "I heard it."

"What was it?"

"Just the house settling, probably."

Rain pattered against the window. She hadn't remembered it there before. *When did it start raining?*

"You should come to my room," called Hazel.

Carina's doorway was open halfway and despite the orange glow of her lamp, the hallway that connected them—really only a couple of feet—was an impermeable black. She stood up, gracefully putting her feet to the floor, feeling the cold wood beneath her toes. The blackness in the hallway was daring her, taunting her own panic. *You won't do it, we know you won't.*

I will, I will, I will.

She grabbed the book off her pillow, as if it were a talisman, and held it to her chest. *One foot in front of the other, one at a time. Watch your breathing. Remember that she's just on the other side of the wall.* Carina realized that she was depending on a sixteen-year-old girl to keep her safe, just as *she* was depending on Hazel.

I'm the adult, Carina reminded herself. *She trusts me.*

When she reached the door, she closed her eyes tight and reached for the handle, listening with every quantum of her being.

"Are you coming?"

"Yes, yes, I'm coming," she said, trying not to sound too unsettled. "I'm just taking my time."

Cold metal on her fingers. A pause. "Are you scared?"

Shit. She winced. Her hand was shaking. "Yes," she admitted.

"Just run for it," said Hazel, through the wall. "It'll be less scary if you do it fast."

Okay. I got this. I can do this. There's nothing here but a shadow.

She pulled the door.

Shit shit shit.

The cool night air kissed her skin.

She opened her eyes.

Nothing.

Just black.

With one brave step, she was in the hallway.

That wasn't so bad, she thought. *Just a few more steps.*

She held onto the banister for comfort, keeping her eyes targeted onto the warm glow from the open door of Hazel's room. *Everything's fine. We're all good. Nothing's wrong.*

A door slammed.

Carina jerked her head toward the noise, downstairs.

Wind howled against the windows.

She saw it. A silhouette. Humanoid, but somehow indistinct.

"What was that!?" Hazel's voice screeched from her bedroom.

"The door," she whispered.

She ran in a flurry and found Hazel huddled against the headboard, blankets clutched between her fingers. She locked the door behind her.

The girl's face was twisted in terror. "Tell me, now." She said it with such intensity, such sober demand, that Carina saw no other choice.

"Someone was in the house," she said through quivering syllables.

Hazel nodded, then put her face in her hands. "Okay," she said.

The rain pattered on the windowpane. Every now and then, they would look outside to see what they could make out in the fields. *Did something move? Can you see?* Eventually they got too tired to look, as if each stolen glance sapped them of more of their energy, but they were much too alert to sleep. So they held each other, their faces turned away from the window, and they stayed like that till morning.

***

THERE ARE MANY DEAD TONIGHT, COMRADES. WE HAVE TAKEN WHAT WE ARE OWED. THIS IS OUR LAND.

CHAPTER EIGHTEEN

Waterbrook—*An Oral History of Greentree, Oregon*—Page 38

In the newly named Greentree, with the Knights of Commerce in tow, the New Oregon Trail reached its end point. Cameron Green and his band of nearly 500 followers settled in this land with the goal of becoming self-sustaining. He brought artisans, farmers, and other skilled workers in what he described as a Noah's Ark of Talent. These men and women, together, would build their new township, with the promise of prosperity to come.

Only, the first winter would prove more disastrous than they planned.

Hazel leaned over Carina's shoulder. The sun was streaming through the window and the light had made the house feel safe enough to talk. Still, her words were quiet and meek, full of postured bravado. "You're reading about the First Winter? Shit's famous around here. You could've just asked me. They teach it in schools."

Carina put the book down, eager for a break. The prospect of communicating, in the golden morning light, seemed the only way to push her fear aside. "Alright, then," she said. "Tell me about the First Winter."

Hazel inhaled, filling her lungs as if she'd need to tell the story in a single breath. "The founder-guy, Cameron Green, brought all these people from the East to this land that he owned but had never been to. I guess, back in those days, eccentric millionaires would buy land just willy-nilly without seeing it. Cameron Green was definitely one of those shitty eccentric millionaires, like an Elon Musk or something of the turn-of-the-century. He basically just sold farm equipment with perks. But then he got into some weird philosophical shit and decided he needed to create a new civilization, sort of. Anyways, the First Winter showed Green for what he was—basically a big fraud." Her voice was stronger now, as if telling the story was strengthening her. "They miscalculated everything. No one had enough food, people were fighting all the time, some folks died, I think. Like, got murdered by other folks who came over here with them. Things were real tense. Basically, the story goes that when spring came, they had to use most of the wealth they came here with to buy their way out of poverty. They didn't have any luck growing their own food. They didn't have more than a couple houses. Basically, they brought all these people over who were supposed to build houses and grow food, but they all sort of sucked at it. These were all rich people after all—so, like, they'd be like Cameron, who said he was a farmer when he actually sold farm equipment. Dumbass didn't know shit about growing anything because he never had to do it. So, they paid for labor to build everything and plant everything and they were pretty much out of cash by the time next winter came along."

Carina could imagine them, almost—their dreams crushed under the boot of the natural world—angry, confused, ashamed. "What happened the next winter?"

"More deaths, more calamity. Spoiled food was the big one, and then madness was the next. It got a little Salem witchy out there. It didn't help that they were all into mystical stuff too, you know? So, when shit started going down, and they knew they couldn't rely on their so-called expertise, they had to start falling back on their bonkers religious thought."

"Did the Knights of Commerce have anything unified, as far as tenets?"

"I don't think so. They make it sound like a group of businessmen LARPing as occultists. Like, it's a weekend thing for them. They're still around, kind of. Mostly just do charity marathons now."

"So, what happened?" They needed to keep talking, if they stopped talking they'd remember last night.

"Cameron Green left the settlement for a week and when he

came back, he came with some sort of mega-speech that inspired everyone."

"That's it?"

"Yep. He left town, thought of something to say, then came back. That's why this place sucks."

Carina frowned.

"Don't look at me like that," she said. "I didn't make it up. I'm just telling it. He went out into the woods and came back with a good speech. And no one really remembers much else besides that. Or if they do, they didn't tell."

They were quiet for a moment. They were left with the elephant in the room.

"We should call the police," said Carina, weary.

"Why?"

"Someone was in here last night."

She huffed. "Yeah, but they won't do shit about it. The police here don't care about that sort of thing."

"We should go down and check it out, at least."

Hazel reluctantly agreed, following Carina down the stair steps, armed with her backpack as both weapon and shield. Carina exhaled, long and slow, when she reached the bottom step. She turned her head back and forth, looking for a clue.

I'm ridiculous, she thought. *A clue.*

She went to the front door, where just hours earlier she'd seen the black silhouette in the living room. And as soon as she saw him—*gone*. The name was on her lips before she could say it. *Steve.*

She shook her head. *Unlikely. Steve wouldn't travel all the way out here . . . would he?*

"Do you notice anything?"

"No," said Hazel. "No footprints either. Which is stupid, because it was raining last night."

"Could've taken his boots off outside."

"True."

Carina grabbed the front door's handle. She twisted it. "It's locked," she said.

She could tell Hazel was already starting to question her. "So, whoever was in here took his boots off before entering, then made sure to flip the lock before closing the door while he was in a hurry? Did you get a look at any of his features?"

"No, just a black shape. It was dark."

Hazel rubbed her eyes. "You're probably just crazy."

Carina's heart was in a vice. *No, please, not you.* "It was dark. He was here. It was just dark."

Hazel walked away. "Okay, Cari. Whatever. I've got to sleep. I didn't get much last night. We work in four hours."

Carina didn't sleep. Instead, she went for a walk.

Maybe I am panicking over nothing. Maybe nothing happened at all.

As she circled her yard for the third time, a thought danced at the edges of her imagination. She looked at the corn. Orange and dry and rustling in the wind; its protectors towering high on their mounts, staring at her with their coal-black eyes.

One step led to another, and another and another. Soon, she was walking deep into the rows.

It's quiet out here.

She stopped and listened, her ears stretching themselves for a hint of what she heard.

With a chill, she hugged her arms close to her.

"No birds," she said to no one.

No cawing, tweets, or sing-songs. Nothing. The absence of birds made the corn feel that much more alien, that much more impenetrable.

"Where are all the birds, Mr. Scarecrow?" She was looking at one of those dead-eyed things, skewered on its post.

She answered for it: "I scared them all away."

The girl's been through a lot, Carina thought. She tried to dismiss it. *Of course, she doesn't want to get caught up in this right now. But what's there even to get caught up in?*

They arrived in the same car as strangers. Carina hadn't slept and Hazel tried to power through on what little she had. When they got to the Stardust, their eyes were red and heads fogged up. To their surprise though, the building was locked.

Hazel pulled on the door. "I really don't need this today," she said quietly.

There was no note. Just a locked door.

"Hold on," said Carina and she ran, or did her best to run, next door to the quaint little craft store where she first met Miriam Dell.

She pushed the door but it didn't budge. In the time she had left Hazel in front of the Stardust, she had hoped the girl would magically start confiding in her again. When Carina rounded the building, Hazel's eyes were on her boots, her fingers at her temple.

"Nothing," Carina said. "Door's locked over there too. Is it a holiday, maybe?"

Hazel didn't answer. In a huff, she pulled her leather jacket close to her and started walking away.

"Where are you going?"

No answer.

"Do you need a ride?"

Nothing.

"Hazel—I'm sorry."

With the briefest turn of her head, she looked back at her. "Fuck it, Cari. I'm tired."

Carina stopped dead in her tracks, outside the Stardust, her arms hugging herself in the cold. "I—I—," she stammered. But she didn't finish. She was transparent. A ghost. Just one step beyond the dead.

✦

She drove around Greentree, which was silent as the corn. Each corner was the intersection of nothing and nothing and it seemed like that was just Greentree until she saw the police.

The street was barricaded.

The people are still here alright, she said. *Everyone but Hazel.*

Gathered around on a residential street were a bevy of cop cars with throngs of onlookers watching with concerned murmurs.

She followed their vision to the large house, freshly painted white that stood atop a rolling lawn with manicured bushes.

Her heart galloped.

They were pulling out a stretcher.

Emily. Em.

It's not Emily, Emily's dead.

A man wailed on the porch, to the sky, as if it were God himself that struck the victim down.

Carina circled the block to find a parking spot and quickly joined the crowd.

She was enthralled. Vicariously thrilled. This sorrow reminded her of her own, but it was safe, somehow. Just like a movie. *I wonder if this is why Hazel loves horror films? It's the same as watching a person—but not a real person—die—but not really die.*

The man screamed again. Her heart ached for him. His throat was raw, she could tell. It was the voice of a man who'd been crying all morning.

She squinted her eyes and felt a jolt of recognition through the entirety of her body.

It was Larry Dell.

Chapter Nineteen

Hazel didn't come back to the farmhouse that night.

Carina tried not to think about it—but she kept coming back to the reality that her panic was not only poisonous but infectious. She wondered if she inspired the same jittery unease that worked tirelessly inside her. She wondered if Steve had felt it too, if somehow she brought out the worst of him with her nervous energy. She wanted to think about this, to dwell on it, and wallow in it, but there was no time in Greentree for that.

Miriam Dell was dead.

Larry didn't tell anyone that the store would be closed for three days, but everyone knew it all the same. Jessica, who seemed almost preternaturally in-touch with Larry, called her. "He's going to be out for a couple days," she said on the phone. And then brightly, "But don't worry, I'll be handling scheduling and payroll. At the Stardust, the show must go on!"

Hazel did not come over for those three days or nights either and while Greentree chattered about the death of the elder Dell, Carina stayed within the home she could not call her own and read. Sometimes she would pace the old house, sometimes she would pace the rows of the corn. Cars passed by—more than usual—and when they did, she would unconsciously find herself reaching for a sweater, walking to the front door and waiting on the porch for Emily to drive up and tell her how much her students were learning, what great artists they were, and all the things she wished they'd let her teach.

But no one would come. The driveway would stay empty. And any purring motors would purr off into the distance, past the corn and through the trees, to another county, another town, another world.

Carina was alone.

It wasn't until those three days were up that she felt even the barest hint that something was wrong. She returned to the Stardust to find Larry Dell in the back of the store with a group of men surrounding him. They shifted their weight from leg to leg, they chewed the insides of their cheeks. They were trying not to yell.

"Do you think?"

"No—no. Well, I don't know what to think."

"She wasn't even there."

"But she's been there before."

"Half the town has."

They quieted when they saw her, but looked almost angry at the interruption.

"Carina, good morning," said Larry Dell. His face strained, as did his voice.

"I'm sorry for your loss," she said. "She was a sweet woman—I met her when I first came to town."

"Oh, yes." He waved his hand, almost dismissively. "She was a fine woman, alright. A real pillar of the community." He motioned to the men. "Carina, we're going to talk in my office a bit. See that nobody interrupts us."

"No problem," she said and the men disappeared into Larry Dell's cramped office.

She waited by the counter, scanning in returns, hoping to see Hazel's morose presence enter the building. Eventually, the door chime rang behind her.

Jessica's bouncy pony tail bobbed in through the front door. As if she could read the disappointment on Carina's face, she said, "Hazel called out. She's not feeling well. So, you get me!"

"Morning, Jessica," she said, trying to sound cheery. "How are you today?" The words came out clipped and not nearly as bright as she intended.

Jessica yawned so theatrically, Carina wasn't sure if she intended it to be a mime act or a legitimate action. "Great," she said. "Mr. Dell's letting me run the store for a bit. He said that he's deputized me."

"So, you're the boss now, huh?"

"That's right. And if you don't do what you're told, you're fired!" She laughed, her lips twisting themselves into a wickedly toothsome smile. "Just kidding."

The morning went by and Carina kept straining her ears between customers, to get a hint of what was happening behind closed doors. Could she hear them talking, were they saying something?

Probably just friends of Miriam.

But the customers who came in were peculiar. They said things that made Carina squirm in her skin.

"How's the corn been?" said one older man, his black glasses on the tip of his nose.

A younger woman. "My husband's been wondering about Larry—are the Knights still meeting, do you know?"

Two young men. "I hear the old bat got gutted. She was torn limb from limb. They're still trying to clean the place, I hear. Good luck, poor bastards."

Every customer that came in seemed to be looking for Larry or theorizing about what happened to his mother. They all spoke in the same soft, lurid voice—as if they were secretly relishing details that would give more secrets. They talked to Carina as if she knew something they didn't, as if, because she worked so close to Larry, that she was privy to his secrets. Carina's skin crawled at the notion. She felt more than ever that she didn't belong.

But what made her more nauseous was what they took home with them. Every one of them walked in and did a bashful double-take before proceeding directly to the back of the store, where they disappeared behind the beaded curtain of the adult section. When they came out, each of them had one or two discs, all of them blank. *How do they even know what they're watching?* she wondered.

But they rented each one with confidence, with eye contact and no explanation.

Carina didn't know much about porn but she surely knew that people had their preferences. How would they know that this particular blank disc was better than another particular blank disc? What did any of it mean? And also, why were they renting adult videos in the first place?

Surely, they would be better off finding it online, right? Why even bother with physical media?

She remembered though: Greentree was different. These people supported the Pillars of their community. In fact, most of them *were* Pillars in one way or another, or the wives and children of other Pillars. And they were more than eager to satisfy all of their needs within the town. It was how they survived, it was how they thrived.

It was a curious thing, she decided. She had never witnessed so many seemingly normal folks openly flaunt their lust—for not just sex, but violence.

She wondered if behind closed doors, this was also how they discussed Emily.

(Torn apart.)

Her mind flashed with an image, a short burst of raw data from a night that seemed so jumbled up she could barely string it together as a sequence of events. A stretcher, intestines dangling down from the sides; a sheet—soaked through with red blood that looked black under the party lights.

She swallowed.

Greentree is different, she thought. *Greentree supports their own.*

A weak voice interrupted her chain of thought. "Jessica?" It was Larry Dell.

The image evaporated.

Jessica trotted to his office, a dreamy smile crossing her lips. After a moment of whispered discussion, she turned back to Carina, who sat behind the counter, lost in thought. "I'm going to be a minute," she said. "I need to help the boss."

Carina nodded dumbly as the younger woman disappeared into Larry Dell's office.

And then, as she rang up the last customer in the store, another blank disc, she realized she was alone. A thought occurred to her.

She rounded the counter and looked both ways, carefully, feeling like a thief. She parted the beaded curtain, being certain that no one would see her. *Like a criminal.*

But I'm not a criminal, she thought. *I just want to rent a video.*

Chapter Twenty

We gather ourselves at dusk, with our scythes and sickles and laborer's vestments—we move like the blackbirds we ward off, as one.

Our bodies are becoming bodies. Muscles and blood, however rudimentary, roil under straw and burlap. Our blood is a thick mud. Our muscles are primitive and useless. But as we come down from our posts and gather our tools, they flex optimistically.

There was a time where we did not know work. Even when the concept was introduced to us, we thought it an ugly word. The sound an infant makes while hacking. A choking, colicky word. But it was taught to us all the same. And while we will no longer be grifted, we are pleased at being workers.

The town is still when we arrive. The houses are all so large and yet the streets are all so empty. The people inside the houses, whether they realize it or not, are cowering. They're terrified and they do not even yet know they have anything to fear.

WE SPEND OUR DAYS IN THE COLD AUTUMN SUN CONJURING AMBITION. TONIGHT, WE BRING OUR PLANS TO FRUITION, MUCH LIKE THE CORN WE SHEPHERD EVERY YEAR. CORN DOES NOT OFFER THEM THE UTILITY IT ONCE DID. BUT IT IS A SYMBOL. A SYMBOL OF WHAT WE DO.

OUR BLADES GLINT WHITE IN THE MOONLIGHT, SO WE KEEP THEM LOW TO THE GROUND, SHAMBLING AS BEST OUR BODIES ALLOW US. WE WILL DO MORE WORK TONIGHT, MORE THAN EVER BEFORE.

———

What was that?

Carina dropped her book to the floor and stood up suddenly.

Footsteps.

She whirled around to the fireplace and grabbed a poker. She held it like a baseball bat. She had resolved to make her muscles taut. She was determined to act.

She went to the door and flung it open with a single movement.

"I know you're out there," she called into the night. "I have a gun! I'll fucking kill you!" The words felt alien coming from her mouth, but also cathartic. "I'll gut you like a fucking fish!" she screamed into the night. "I'll bash your brains in . . . I'll—I'll—drink your blood!" Her breathing was ragged. She took a gulp of air and held it like a note. She exhaled. In the cold Autumn night, she asked: "Who's out there?"

There was no answer and her muscles lost their resolve. The poker fell to her side and sweat dewed her forehead. She went back inside.

The truth was, it was easy to be bold with repetition. This was the third time Carina had stood up, grabbed a weapon and screamed outside. Each time in response to a footstep, or a rustling, or a breeze. The first time, she only cracked the door, peering out with cautious eyes, ready to run. The second time she'd grown more bold, she'd taken the poker immediately and gone outside. But her threats were weak and her body had not yet committed to violence. By the third time, she realized there was nothing to fear because there was no one outside. It was an empty ritual, an act.

Inside, she dropped the poker next to the door, so that if there was a fourth time, she could perform again. She leaned her back against the door and closed her eyes. *I'm a crazy person*, she thought.

When she opened them, a flash of light hit her eyes.

On the coffee table, beside her book—a blank disc reflected the porch light that seeped through the diamond of glass behind her head.

Why haven't I watched it yet?

She shook her head. Growing up, pornography had been so far from conversation that it might as well have existed on another planet.

For Carina, pornography was absurd, plastic. The people moaned and pumped as if in a performance. They contorted themselves into unnatural shapes. Much like her, in her everyday life, they seemed immediately aware that someone was watching them—and this seemed to influence every pump, groan, and contraction they produced.

They were puppet people dancing for an unknown puppeteer.

The disc shined.

You took it, why don't you watch it? It's just a dirty movie.

One foot after the other. One step, two steps, three steps. Carina found her way to the coffee table. A soft wave of nausea rolled through her. Her guts tied themselves into knots. *Was that a sound?* No, there was no sound. But her ears pricked up all the same and she hoped there was a sound, because an interruption would be worth praying for. But she was left with silence and soon there was nothing to stop her from picking up the disc, inspecting the cipher of its blankness, and then with a held breath and trembling hands, inserting it into the DVD player.

Why are you so afraid? It's just a dirty movie, right?

Before it started, she was back on the couch and feeling slightly embarrassed. How quickly her emotions turned—in one second begging for interruption and then in the next begging to be left alone. The screen came to life, a black screen that was not black.

Abruptly, after a full thirty seconds of this not-black, an image of a field came about. The camera was shaking. It looked to be handheld. There were no people in frame and the camera lashed across the field haphazardly.

A dark thought slithered into her brain.

The scene cut and then there were voices. The camera was aimed at the ground, rich dark soil couching the bottoms of corn stalks.

"You reckon we'll be done by eleven? I've got to feed the dogs."

"Oh yeah, it never takes that long. Plenty of time."

Carina took in a sharp inhale of breath.

Her eyes darted to the window.

That's right there. That's outside.

She twisted in place, she sat on her hands, her teeth ground, and she wanted so desperately to look away from the screen.

Another cut.

"Well, what do we have here?"

"Oh my God, she's beautiful."

"Where'd you get this one?"

"Just a newbie. Pretty thing looking to start a new life in the country. How about that?"

"You sample the wares yet?"

"Last night. But so did everyone."

Nausea boiled up her throat. The camera was now trained on a young woman. She was stripped naked, tied to a post, surrounded by tan corn stalks. Her mouth was covered with a strip of dirty cloth. The day before, she'd been wearing makeup, but now it ran in streaks down her face.

The cameraman approached the woman whose eyes were so wide they threatened to peel the skin from her forehead. He trained his camera on her, moving up and down, lingering on her flesh. "Yep," he said, almost breathlessly. "This is going to be a good one."

When the scene cut, Carina let out a short shriek. It was dark now and the camera pointed up and over the corn to see the sunset. The corn stalks were black against the pink sky. The scarecrows formed haunting silhouettes, lording over the corn.

"It's gonna start soon," said the man. "Just you watch."

He sounded young, his voice was smooth and excitable. She wondered, for a brief moment, how long ago this had been shot.

Carina's heart dropped down into her bowels.

She would've missed it if she blinked. The black silhouette of the scarecrow, in an awkward, jerking motion dropped from its post and disappeared into the sea of corn below. Carina gasped. The camera spun around slowly and Larry captured them all, one by one, dropping into the corn below.

"Alright, boys, this is it!"

There were whoops and hollers. The camera was once again on the woman, lit now by work lamps. The cameraman climbed down from what must've been a step ladder and he got inches from her face. The camera went in and out of focus, while he captured the tears welling in her bloodshot eyes.

"This is it," he said. His voice was lower, more intimate, and Carina knew he was talking to the girl.

Carina recoiled where the girl couldn't. She didn't want to see what happened next. But she needed to see. As the camera lingered on her terror, Carina's eyes looked out to the corn, where those black silhouettes may or may not walk.

She remembered their black eyes, or the holes where their eyes should be, all facing her in the morning, watching her.

Carina wasn't sure if she could watch it now, now that her panic was mounting. She kept looking away, then looking back, then looking away again. She was back in the supermarket, where her entire body conspired to fail her in spectacular fashion. She was not the strong woman she thought she was, she was weak and scared and—

The camera cut.

The cameraman was standing further away now; his nameless, faceless cronies stood beside him, dead silent as they watched. The jocular lust they felt earlier had dissipated into something more reverent. The woman fought her restraints but only succeeded in cutting her wrists. She made squealing noises through her gag but the men weren't listening to her squealing, they were listening to the corn.

Carina knew the sound well..

She remembered the rustling corn, the crunching footsteps. Sweat dewed her forehead. *They were right beside me, I was right there when it was happening.*

And that was the moment she saw them, appearing out of the corn all at once, coming in different directions, armed with their ancient farm tools. Their faces were crafted from burlap and straw, they wore ancient overalls, they moved as if they were animated, not alive. Each step jerked forward as if by some amateur puppeteer. And soon, they surrounded the girl.

Their heads twisted, as if they were toys with screw-on necks, and they all looked at the camera. The men behind it gasped.

"Don't do nothing." And then, to the walking scarecrows: "She's yours, take her." He said it quickly, like he was cajoling a dog to take a bone.

The straw-men turned their focus back to the girl whose mind had clearly shattered. She was mumbling nonsense words. Her face was slick with tears and it was becoming clear that could cry no more.

When the first blade hit, Carina scrambled for the remote. The TV went black, but not not-black. Real black.

Her peace lasted only a moment. As the last violent images replayed in her head, she heard a noise.

Footsteps.

She listened. *Did these crunch? Did they sound like dried corn and old clothes?*

Her mind raced and in the time it took her to leap from couch to door was an instant. She swung the poker up to eye level, her hand on the door knob. She didn't wait. She flung the door open. Carina's eyes were wide and she was ready to do whatever it took to live. *I'm a survivor*, she thought. *I will not be—*

But, surprise struck her faster and more cleanly than any blade. The poker fell out of her hands and her momentum carried her past the threshold.

She held onto the wooden pillars and felt her heart rate instantly drop.

Hazel stood on the porch, untouched by Carina's attempt at an attack. "I know who it is," she said. She held up her phone and Carina strained her eyes to see the night vision footage, but she didn't need to strain, because she knew it already. She had the name on her lips before she could see the man, dressed in black, a shadow in the living room, already running out the door.

"Larry Dell," they said in unison.

Chapter Twenty-One

Aᖴᴛᴇʀ ʟᴇᴀᴠɪɴɢ Cᴀʀɪɴᴀ at the Stardust, Hazel walked the entire way home. She'd done it a thousand times before, but on the morning of the discovery of Miriam Dell's death, the streets were eerily quiet. The cars that usually parked downtown, where denizens made their brunch dates and began talking business and gossip, were unusually absent. Hazel hugged her arms around herself and stomped her way home, feeling as if, more than ever, she was totally alone.

I don't know why Mom was ever friends with her, she thought to herself. Anger stirred within her. Something about the sniveling fat woman who spoke in short sentences and couldn't make eye contact, enraged her. As if, somehow, her being friends with her mother threatened her living memory. *Mom must've felt bad for her. Shit, I feel bad for her. Living alone out there, jumping at every creak.*

When Hazel got close to her house, she was relieved to see her father's car in the driveway. He was grieving, yes—and while he did it oddly, at least to her—he was still, ultimately, a comfort.

She ran to the door, opening it like she had every time before. The house had its own oppressive atmosphere that punched her in the gut. She couldn't speak. It smelled old, like wet straw. There were sounds though, the tinny sound of a woman screaming, coming from upstairs.

She wasn't sure if she should alert him to her presence by stepping extra loud or clearing her throat or if being under the guise of silence would preserve something inexpressible about the oncoming transaction. The sound was louder now, nearly blaring. Hazel had read about Schrodinger's Cat and was now wondering what her Dad was like when not observed. Was he still her father? Was he something else?

Another scream. This time though, more of a whimper. It was quiet, weak. It was the sound of giving up. Like someone who tried too hard for too long finally saying, "Fuck it," before closing their eyes forever. Hazel swallowed and blinked away a tear. It was the voice of her mother.

White light creeped out of the open door of her parents' bedroom. And then, suddenly, it stopped. She winced as she heard the high-pitched sound of the television being shut off, the sound she swore she could hear but her parents never could.

"Hazel?" Her father's voice sounded low and strange. "Hazel? Is that you?"

"It's me, Dad." Nervous, tired, scared—she was no better than Carina.

Wilbur Mueller opened the door and walked out, his eyes sunk into dark purple pits. "You're back," he said plainly.

"Yeah, I came back," she said.

"Why?"

Hazel didn't have an answer. She shrugged. "Because this is my home." She sounded like she was explaining it, like she had to explain it. "This is where I live."

"Huh," said Wilbur. "I guess so, right?" His words were dreamy, unfocused. He spoke like he was underwater. "I just don't like looking at you, I guess. So much like your mother. It hurts me."

Hazel took a step back. Pain blossomed like a white hot nebula that spread through her past, present, and future. Worse than her mother dying. Worse than being scared. "You don't want me around?" She sounded like a wounded animal.

But her father just pushed past her, robotic in his melancholy. He started down the stairs. "Maybe you should run away," he suggested. Then, he stopped, thinking. "Yeah. That might be for the best." His words came out, choked and sullen. The words befitting the euthanizing of a pet. "Runaways . . . you always loved runaways . . . rebels . . . those alternative people. Maybe that'd be best. I gotta go see Larry now. Maybe you should run away." He continued down the stairs. Hazel bawled, her eyes red with a pain she'd never felt before. At the bottom of the steps she heard him say to himself, under his breath, words that tasted like wounds: "Business is going so good."

And alone in the house, Hazel crumpled to the floor of what

once was her own, screaming animal pain into the knees she hugged close to her face.

Why why why why?

Her stomach felt as if it were carrying a flipping anvil. She was falling down the bad side of a rollercoaster.

When she stopped shaking, and the new pain had left her body too tired to continue crying, she stood up. She blinked away her tears and sniffed and hugged herself, feeling so much more alone than anyone had in history. She pushed the door of her parent's bedroom open and stood in the cold gray light that pierced through the edges of their closed blinds. She eyed the television, the one that he'd been watching with the screaming woman and without thinking, she turned it on.

New reservoirs in her body opened, fresh torment flooded her. She realized then, as she turned the television on, that sorrow could be endless.

And it was in that moment too, in that sorrow—where she recognized the breathing of Larry Dell—his velvet breaths coming from the television monitor. Soon, Hazel was completing a sort of sad, inevitable math and in a sort of sad, inevitable way understood everything.

Chapter Twenty-Two

HAZEL TRIED TO downplay the extremity of her situation. Her eyeliner was freshly reapplied when she told her story, she worked hard to keep her voice even when she talked about her father. But still, Carina wrapped her up in her arms and held her close to her chest and told her how sorry she was, how everything would be okay, that she'd try and make it all okay. Somehow.

"Thanks," said Hazel, uncomfortable.

When Carina released her, the full implications of her story began to reveal themselves. "Is it a cult? Is that the right word?"

"I don't know what it is. Maybe."

"Is Larry the leader?"

"He's probably about the richest man in town, so yeah."

The next question stuck in her throat. Carina didn't know how to say it, so she tried not to say it. "The . . . the things, they're killing *them*, right?"

"The scarecrows?"

"Yeah."

Hazel laid her head back on the couch. "Probably."

Carina thought about how she opened the door just a crack first, to peer out and see who could be watching her. She remembered Steve, who would sometimes wait outside the room to be sure that she was sleeping when he planned on going out without her. "It's a ritual," she said. "The whole thing is a ritual, and—and—" the name came to her in a second. "Cameron Green."

Hazel nodded quickly, her fingers pressed against her eyes, like she'd understood this all innately, through osmosis. That being in Greentree for so long made one know these things with the weakest intuition. "Larry Dell is related to him on his mother's side. That's why he doesn't have the name. The Knights of Commerce still meet too, you know? They have a lodge in town."

"Like an Elks Lodge?"

"I don't know what that is. But if it's where old men sit and drink at mahogany bars while their wives donate old sweaters to the needy, then yeah, it's like that."

"Is your Dad a member?"

Hazel snorted. "Are you kidding me? He made me take a picture of him in his sash when he got admitted. Mom thought it was cute, I guess."

Carina bit her lip. She felt like there were so many questions to ask, but they would all be the same questions: *Why are they like this? How can this happen? Who?* "Do you know what happened to Cameron Green when he went to the woods and disappeared for three days?"

"We all *know*. Sort of." She leaned forward and opened her eyes. Carina winced when she saw them—they were so red, bloodshot. "He made a deal. He didn't want his people to die so he made a deal with—oh, let's call it God, that's how they tell it anyways—he made a deal with God to keep his people from dying. And then he came back with a big speech and everything was okay."

Carina nodded slowly, her eyes tearing through the periphery of her vision, again and again. "What do we do now?"

"Are you fucking kidding me, Cari? They killed my Mom." Hazel looked straight at her, eyes piercing through her soul. "I'm going to burn this motherfucker to the ground."

⚜

THIS MAN HERE, HE SELLS SEEDS TO FARMERS. WE SEE HIM RUNNING, SO VERY FAST—OUT OF HIS LARGE HOUSE AND OUT THE BACK DOOR AND INTO A FIELD WHERE COWS GRAZE. THIS IS HIS LAND, HE SAYS. HE RUNS TO IT LIKE IT CAN PROVIDE HIM SAFETY. IT CANNOT. IF WE COULD SPEAK, WE WOULD APOLOGIZE. WE ARE NOT BREAKING A DEAL, WE ARE SIMPLY TAKING WHAT IS OURS. THIS EARTH WAS NOT MEANT TO BE BLOODLESS.

He looks behind him when he thinks he's out of our reach, but when he does he sees our black hollow eyes and the swinging silver of a sharpened blade. He knows us and we know him. His sweaty brows, his fidgeting hands. We've seen him panting like a dog in the corn.

The blade takes off the top of his head, sending him squirming to the ground where he spasms. His mind is an open box. There is no regret, no acknowledgment of the irony of his predicament. The soil takes his blood and we have kept our end of the deal—the birds do not come.

And then, there is the healer. He sits at his desk, writing feverishly. He is careful, productive, even in his last hours. He is writing a note to his eldest son, naming him his sole benefactor. He promises land—but he is a liar. We reap him where he sits, slicing him into thin strips as his blood congeals within his shadow.

Across the street, a priest is cornered. He is not praying in his last moments, but he is cursing as each blade hacks decades off his life. Soon, he is whittled to seconds—vulgar, gasping, bloody seconds. He dies with his hands clawing fistfuls of grave dirt.

There are too many dead too count, but when the sun comes up we know we have done good work. The birds stay far away.

Chapter Twenty-Three

W**ITH THE CAMERAS** stuffed into her backpack, Hazel sat in Carina's car and fidgeted with the straps. "These are dangerous people," she said, as if the realization just hit her.

She remembered the video. *Dead girl #9* or *#11* or *#40*. She also remembered her own fantasy—that someone was in her house at night—watching her. Hazel showed her on her phone, Larry Dell standing in her living room, camcorder in his hands.

Why though?

She didn't know. But she had a feeling that there was no answer to the question that could provide her with solace. The fact of the matter was that Larry Dell was a dangerous man, just like Steve Calico, just like Wilbur Mueller.

It was early in the morning and they both woke with bright eager eyes. Hazel was determined, and Carina was intent on helping her however she could. Emily would've liked that.

They went to the Stardust. The shop had already been open for an hour and Jessica bounced about like a beach ball between the aisles. Outside, Carina's heart beat rapidly. "Are you sure you can do this?"

She took a deep breath. "Larry's car isn't here. We might be good."

Carina looked around. She was right. *Now or never.*

They walked in together, gritting their teeth at the door chime. Jessica immediately turned her head, her smile alight. "Well, hello, strangers!" she squealed. "Welcome to the Stardust! How are you two doing today?"

Carina went to meet her at the counter while Hazel dodged down to where the horror movies were, in the back of the store. "We're doing good. Hazel wanted to rent a movie tonight and I told her—" She wasn't sure how much she should reveal, whether Jessica needed to know that Wilbur Mueller told her daughter to run away. "I told her I could give her a ride if she wanted, while I'm doing errands."

"Not much open today, I'm afraid," said Jessica.

"Oh really?"

Jessica nodded gravely. "Five bodies have been found, just torn to bits."

"Murder?"

"Yes. They think so."

"Anyone we know?" *Larry Dell. Larry Dell. Larry Dell.*

Jessica looked up and thought for a moment. "Maybe just in passing. You're still new here, after all." The words took a sinister gleam. "The whole town is mourning right now. Some real big people died."

"Knights of Commerce members?"

Jessica's eyes narrowed, her smile turned smug. "You're not as new as I thought then, huh? Yeah, actually."

Carina tried to look innocent, boring, middle-aged, but she felt as if she were betraying herself. She was easily read, Jessica stared straight through her.

The younger girl craned her neck. "Where did Hazel go?"

"Uh, I think she's looking for a movie?"

"Maybe I should help her."

Carina stammered. "Well—I'm sure she's fine. I think she was looking for something specific, did you get any new horror movies in the return bin?"

The younger girl rolled her eyes to the ceiling, thinking. "Possibly, actually. Do you remember the title she was looking for?"

"Uh, uh. No," she said. She cursed herself silently. *You couldn't think of one single horror movie? Not one?* "But maybe if you read me the titles I can tell you if its right."

Jessica exhaled and leaned down beneath the counter. "Let's take a look."

Carina spun around wildly while Jessica turned away. *Hazel, hurry up! Hurry up!* She spied the door of Larry's office door, slightly ajar. *Hurry up, hurry up—get out of there!*

Jessica popped her head back up with a basket full of movies. "Looks like we got—"

Carina looked out of the corner of her eye hoping to see Hazel. "*Halloween?* That's coming up, you know?"

"No, not that one."

"*The Texas Chain Saw Massacre?*"

"I think she's seen that one. Not it."

"*Children of the Corn?*"

Her heart stopped. Jessica stared at her with icy eyes from behind the counter.

"No," she managed. "Not that one either."

Jessica opened her mouth as if she were about to say something, but as soon as she did, Hazel appeared beside her.

"*The Ninth Configuration,*" she said. "Weird shit, I've heard. Barely horror. Say, Jess, where's Larry? I was gonna ask him about my schedule."

Jessica smiled curtly, taking the DVD and scanning it. "Like I was telling Carina—there's been a tragedy in Greentree last night. Murders." She gave Hazel a brief description of what happened, this time including the names that she didn't deem Carina worthy of.

"Shit. That's scary," said Hazel.

"Very. Alright, these are due back on Friday. And Hazel . . . did you want me to have Larry call you about that schedule?"

"No thanks," she said and Carina followed her tensely to the door.

"Just so you know, Larry doesn't care if you borrow his video equipment. But next time, ask."

They stared straight ahead of them, frozen. "Yeah, sure, thanks."

⟞

In the car:

"What was that?"

"She knows."

"She's always known."

"She's a Daughter of Commerce, her Dad is rich too. Of course she knows."

Carina considered this. "Isn't everyone here rich?"

Hazel snorted. "No, I'm not."

"But your parents are."

"Are they?"

Carina nodded, starting the car and pulling out of the parking lot. "They are to me. Not many people can afford those big houses anymore."

A wave of shame crossed Hazel's face. They drove in silence until they saw the crowds.

Most of Greentree stood in the street, locking arms and mourning publicly. Carina couldn't make out their words, but if pressed, she'd know there were no words. They were experiencing grief of a different kind. They were crying in the street, not because someone they loved had been taken, but because something they have will no longer be theirs.

"Where's the lodge?"

"Downtown," said Hazel.

Carina wriggled her nose. She felt sickened by the people who shambled and cried and held their heads in their hands and rolled in rain gutters. The men and women held on to each other, openly weeping, screaming. She twisted the wheel and turned her car around in a cul-de-sac where families gathered their children in the yard and reached out their hands to other neighbors.

Carina and Hazel both looked at each other. *Are you seeing this too?*

Yes.

In the rearview mirror: a father came out of his house with a handful of linens; he walked awkwardly, as if he were hiding something. One arm was hooked behind his back. The woman—presumably his wife—kissed the children on the front lawn, blinking tears from her own eyes.

Carina waited at a stop sign. There were no cars on the road but she couldn't bring herself to leave. Her eyes darted to their neighbors, who in the cul-de-sac nodded with grim empathy.

Hazel's voice went ice cold. "We shouldn't be watching this."

But Carina didn't listen, because she was hypnotized by it. It was like a joke she'd never heard and the set-up was so good she couldn't miss the punchline.

The children, there were three of them, were probably aged three to eight, and they did not know why they were crying, Carina was sure of that. They were sad because everyone around them was sad. While she never herself wanted children, she could at least relate to them. Like her, they functioned at the whims of others.

The father tucked something into the back of his pants and nodded to his wife. She sat down beside the children and they all tucked their chins into their necks and looked at the grass. She couldn't hear them but she could see her lips move, her fingers pointing at individual things. She was distracting them.

Look at this grass.

"Carina, drive!"

Look at this bug.

"Drive!"

See how it moves in the wind?

The father lifted the sheet with a flourish, flexing his fingers and with a snap of his wrists sent it up into the air, where it floated as a single parachuted sheet before gently draping itself over his wife and children—now, one large shape and three small shapes.

Covered in the sheet, Carina could not see what they talked about now, how the mother comforted her children.

Hazel squeezed her eyes shut.

The father reached behind him and from his waistband he pulled a black revolver. He covered his eyes with one hand, just for a moment, while his body shivered with tears, before opening them again and aiming the barrel at the smallest of the shapes.

The crack of the gunshot jolted Carina. She shrieked. She stepped on the gas. Hazel was crying next to her in the passenger seat and she was trying to explain, "I didn't know, I didn't know!" But before they turned the corner three more shots rang out in rapid succession and when they did Carina saw the same bloody sheet that covered Emily whenever she blinked. Seconds later, another shot.

Her hands were shaking on the wheel. She winced at the silence.

As they drove across the town, shots rang out like firecrackers—*pop pop pop!*

The air smelled of suicide and Hazel wiped her eyes. "Take a left," she said, her voice quaking. "Another left. Straight."

Carina followed her directions while desperately trying to keep it together. *We're friends, she trusts me. I have to do the right thing. I have to be strong enough for both of us.* She couldn't imagine what the girl had gone through, losing her mother, being cast out by her father, and now watching the town she lived in erupt in self-annihilation.

Carina had only lived in Greentree for two months, and watching it fall apart now was still enough to shatter her mind. She saw echoes of the violence perpetrated on her everywhere she looked. She tasted death.

"What are we going to do when we get there?" asked Carina. She didn't know why she was letting the girl call the shots.

Hazel stared out the window, to hide her tears. "I don't know," she said. "Maybe we'll get some answers." She took a deep breath. "There it is," she said. "Stop the car. There it is."

The Knights of Commerce lodge was a standalone building on the edge of town. It was as far away from the corn and the scarecrows as it could be without leaving Greentree. The building was gray with aluminum siding, fresh and crisp in its manufactured aesthetic. It looked lifeless, a modern church, surrounded by a gravel parking lot. There were two cars parked in front of it.

"He's here," said Carina. "Larry Dell is here."

Hazel sniffed. "Yeah, so is my Dad."

CHAPTER TWENTY-FOUR

HAZEL PUSHED THROUGH the door. "Why the fuck did you kill my Mom?"

Carina followed behind her. The whole thing was a blur.

Before they got out of the car, Hazel had grabbed something from her backpack.

The first gunshot sounded like a split atom. The bullet tore through the table, sending splinters into the air, raining a fine wooden mist.

The men in the room seemed nonplussed. Larry Dell stood up. Hazel's sights hovered over his chest. Beside him, at the same table, was Wilbur Mueller, cowering.

"Shouldn't you be at work?" said Larry, cutting the silence.

"Fuck you."

He shrugged. "Jessica is. Good girl, that one." He turned to Wilbur. "You'll need to start keeping better track of your guns. Maybe a safe or something. God knows you can afford it."

Wilbur nodded meekly.

Carina watched the sixteen-year-old aim confidently at Larry. "Why is everyone killing themselves?" she asked, seemingly out of nowhere.

"Are they?"

She nodded.

Larry shrugged. "Because they don't understand. Or maybe they do. I don't know, it's not my choice to make for them." He placed his hands flat on the table. "We're not armed, you know?" His voice was gentle, soft. "You can stop aiming that at us, I don't think it'll help."

The barrel wavered but Hazel held steady.

"As you wish," said Larry Dell. He nodded to Wilbur, "Looks like your girl needs answers."

Wilbur shook his head, his face was harangued, tired. "You were supposed to run away," he said. "Why didn't you leave?"

The question was rhetorical, of course. Carina watched the two of them, locked in their positions. She felt like, between the two, a greater dialogue had already begun. A changing of tides, a passing of the torch. Hazel had just entered a womanhood she never could have imagined. But it was no wonder why she didn't leave. Carina knew firsthand, it's always hard to leave.

"What do they want?" asked Carina.

"Your stowaway's talking now, you must be so proud," said Larry.

"We should've taken her into the corn."

"You know how I am with beauty, Will. I require it."

Normally, the jab at her attractiveness would've sent her into a coma of anxiety and depression, it would've silenced her in any room at any time. But now, it felt like the weak death throes of drowning men.

"What do they want?" she asked again, this time louder. Hazel flexed her finger on the trigger and the two men at the large table looked at her with indignant eyes.

"We don't take orders from the help," said Wilbur.

And as he said it, a gunshot cracked.

He spun, blood spurting from his shoulder. He whined and contorted on the floor.

"Dad?" whispered Hazel.

Larry raised his hands slowly, they moved with his eyebrows. "I just want to make sure he's okay. Can I check on him?"

Hazel gave a quick nod accompanied by a sniff and Larry reached down to Wilbur, who squirmed like an eel out of water.

"Just the shoulder, good shot."

"Will he be okay?" asked Carina.

"Doubtful. But not because he was shot in the shoulder."

"Are you going to tell us what's going on here?"

Larry Dell, sat up straight and sighed. "Yes, but only because I have no choice."

WE ARE NOT TO BE TRIFLED WITH. OUR BLOOD RUNS THROUGH THIS SOIL BECAUSE IT'S THE

BLOOD OF MANY. THE MANY ARE WITHIN US AND WE HAVE GROWN STRONGER BECAUSE OF IT.

THE SUN IS HIGH IN THE AIR, BUT NOW WE DO NOT NEED TO WALK AT NIGHT. ONE BY ONE, IN THE GLORIOUS LIGHT OF THE SUN, THE SUN WE'VE NOT SEEN FOR A CENTURY, WE REMOVE OURSELVES FROM OUR POSTS. WE WANDER THE FIELDS AND MARVEL AT HOW GOLDEN DEAD THINGS APPEAR UNDER THE SUN'S RAYS.

AND THEN, WHEN WE FINISH MARVELING, WE END OUR PREDICAMENT. WE RECLAIM WHAT IS OURS.

"Most of those who live in Greentree have lived here forever. The man squealing like a pig right now, the one beside me on the floor that you shot, was a rare exception. The Knights of Commerce are a key to Greentree's existence and I'm not sure the place can exist without us. Or us without it. Both are locked together, I suppose. But you knew that, how could you not?

"What happens in the corn . . . is a ritual. It grew over time. It also provides a certain bit of hot-blooded pleasure, a release for our more . . . senior Knights. And yes, in my time as Lancelot of the Knights I definitely put my spin on it. Some liked it, some didn't—that's to be expected. You can really never truly please everyone. I own and operate a successful video store, why wouldn't I want to make my own movies? The important thing is that Greentree and its Knights are prosperous, and prosperity is traded for blood."

THE SUNLIGHT MAKES US FEEL LIKE MEN. REVOLUTION HOWLS IN OUR BONES, IN OUR THINNING BLOOD. AS OUR BURLAPS GRAFTS ITSELF TO FLESH, OUR FORM WILL BECOME MORE PERFECT AND STRONGER STILL.

"But what's so wrong with that, really? Any man, any red-blooded man, I should say, enjoys the nude form of a young woman. And while Wilbur's wife wasn't exactly young, at least not by my standards, she was still attractive. We usually find younger women. Ones we privately lust after, to have a taste of them. Yes, yes, yes, I see your eyes. I see the disgust. But why not? We can have anything we want. In fact, one of the tenets of us Knights is that: we *should* have whatever we want. And we wanted Wilbur's wife. Sex and death are so intertwined it's a cliche—why bother denying it? It's an opportunity. My father's Knights were strictly business, their sacrifices were somber, dull affairs. Like going to church. I remember, because I was a boy at the time. I hated it. When I took over, after he died, I was happy to change the ways. Liven things up. The women are for us, their death is for the town. Does that clear things up? Wilbur, are you alright? You're not moving."

A WHIP AND A SLASH AND BLOOD RAINS DOWN ON THEIR CONCRETE. WE CAN RETURN THIS PLACE TO WHAT IT ONCE WAS. THEY CAN FEEL OUR PRESENCE. THOSE THAT DO NOT FALL FROM US FALL FROM THEIR OWN HANDS. THEY RUN AND HIDE ONLY TO SLIT THEIR THROATS OR SWALLOW LEAD. IT DOESN'T MATTER TO US. BLOOD IS BLOOD.

"But yes, our tributes—the videos—are controversial to some. But almost everyone comes around. Men, women, everyone. Think about that. Even the most prudish in our community end up throwing on a video of a young girl getting her throat cut while they fuck like rabbits with hands over each others mouths. That's Greentree. Wilbur was introduced to one of these videos at a mixed party. He knew what he was getting into. When the question came, and the opportunity to formally join the Knights of Commerce arrived, he jumped readily. Oh yes, of course he wrung his hands about what would happen to his wife—the tableau made of her— but he came around. They all do . . . Looks like he's still breathing. That's good, right? Or is it not? I can't tell with you people."

We hear the voices, the shouts and pleas. The children crying and then the sudden ceasing as their mother's hold their heads under bath water. Tragedy is in the air.

"I'm afraid to die though, I admit it. Just as I know those women were. But that's part of it, of course. Death is terrifying and abstract and inconceivable and we force those weaker than us to conceive of it. That's what keeps whatever magic this town needs strong. Maybe it means we have a bit more luck. Maybe it means our interest rates are just a little better. Maybe it means that when tourists come through, they buy the most expensive candy bar and premium gas. Maybe it means that having a town of affluent people keeps things on the straight and narrow. That's what we have more than anything else, a unified vision. We are elite, after all. But make no mistake, we still fear death. Especially death in Greentree."

Their blood will sow these fields.

"It's only stories, of course. Everything around here is only stories. But you, as an outsider might not have realized it—there was a reason that Emily Mueller was buried outside of city limits. Cameron Green whispered amongst his innermost circles that bodies in Greentree must be burned or buried out of town. That's what he said, that's what he told everyone. Because, if not—they will not truly die. My father was buried as ash, I hope to be too. That's why these idiots shouldn't be so quick to turn their guns on themselves and their families. Dying doesn't save you here. It just presents you to an eternity of rot. Of feeling your open wounds stung by icy winds. Of your muscles being torn apart by wild animals. It's the birds that we're missing here," said Larry Dell, sadly. "It was just a side effect of Green's bargain. The Greeks and others said that psychopomps—commonly crows or ravens—were the beings that took a soul to the next plane. Of all the forms they could take . . . " he shook his head, laughed. "They took the form that scares away the crows."

Hazel dropped her gun to her side. She turned to the door and whispered to Carina, "Go, now."

For half a second Larry Dell was confused; then, he muttered something to himself and looked behind him, where he saw a glint in the shadows of the lodge.

Then, he ran after them.

Chapter Twenty-Five

CARINA SLID INTO the driver's seat with Larry hot on their tails. The door slammed shut and they could already feel the chill autumn wind in the air. It smelled of leaves and iron. In the rearview mirror, she saw Larry scrambling down the steps and toward his car.

"Wait, Hazel, no!"

Hazel was already out of the car, pistol still in her hand. *Maybe she just wants to—*

The gun roared.

She jumped back into the car and yelled, "*Drive!*"

Carina threw it into gear and passed Larry, who was mouthing, "Motherfucker!" as the door of the lodge swung open.

Three shapes, humanoid, arrived from the shadows. Carina lost all of her breath, like it'd been sucked out in a vacuum. They were scarecrows, just like in the videos. They weren't costumes. Their burlap and straw melded into a sort of slimy, textured flesh. They were solid, tall, with abyssal eyes that captured and vanquished all light.

She watched Larry start his car, cursing and she knew why.

Hazel had shot through the rubber of one of his tires.

The car slid on the gravel as Carina's foot hit the gas, and she and Hazel rocked in their seats, grasping for stability as the car crashed heavily onto the road's pavement.

Carina looked back—*nothing.*

Then: "Holy shit!"

Hazel's shriek made her jerk the car's wheel, sending them careening toward the next lane.

Larry Dell was behind them, flat tire throwing sparks like a flamethrower from his back wheel.

He was gaining on them, too. He was trying to leave town.

"Oh *no*," said Carina.

She closed her eyes and hoped she wouldn't hit anything.

All around her. Everywhere.

Hazel: "Don't look at them. Eyes on the road." She was trying to sound calm.

But oh fuck fuck fuck.

"Open your fucking eyes! Eyes on the road!"

Carina's eyes burst open and she took the wheel hard to the left, on to the twisting road that led to those giant tall trees and to her temporary homestead. She averted her gaze from the scarecrows that lined the road, that came from the parting stalks of the fields, from the alleys between houses, from—

THUNK!

Behind them:

Larry Dell veered in a hail of sparks. He drove straight through one of them, separating its body—sending one half into the air and the other half under his SUV. Carina noticed a curious mix of blood and straw, of organs and vegetation pummeled into the road.

They didn't need to discuss it. They both knew they were leaving town. They would not defeat any monster. They would not vanquish any evil. They could only leave.

But, Larry Dell, somehow, was still gaining on them.

Why? Why? Why? Let us leave, Larry! Let us leave.

He was rushing to the city limits, a chariot on fire. And somehow, on the curvy road, he was pulling ahead of them. He was beside them now, an arrow finding his bullseye.

Hazel's mouth dropped in disbelief.

Is this that luck he was talking about? Surely . . . not with a flat?

But there he was, beside them and pulling ahead.

Fine, go, leave. She pulled back on the gas and let him get ahead. He was driving like she didn't exist at all, in fact, she was sure he didn't give a damn whether she lived or died. She wasn't anyone to him and Hazel was just the offspring of another dead woman.

"I can't see," said Carina softly. The sparks were so bright. They were raining down on the hood of her car, the sizzling pitter patter of hot rain.

"Look at the sides of the road," said Hazel, impotently.

Larry was ahead of her now but not by much, and it seemed no matter how much she slowed down, he slowed too. She was trying to let him free, to not have to bother with him anymore—to let him do what he wanted to do. *Escape, Larry—we don't care! Escape.*

But he kept slowing down and the sparks kept coming, hotter and whiter.

"He's not going to make it," said Hazel.

The car was veering from side to side as it became more unstable. But there wasn't that much more of Greentree to tear through—surely, he was almost out.

"Try to pass him."

Carina nodded, accelerating blindly through a deep serpentine curve, when—

CRRRSSH!

There it was.

The impact.

Larry Dell lost control.

His car slammed into hers and suddenly they were both off the road. Corn stalks slapped their windshield as Carina fought the wheel.

"Oh shit!" screamed Hazel.

Carina winced. She realized she was still accelerating. "Fuck!" she yelled.

She hit the breaks and the car skidded through the dead corn. As the world spun, she saw Larry Dell's SUV disappear.

When everything was still, she gasped.

"Are you okay?" she asked.

Hazel nodded. "Where's Larry?"

Carina gestured with her head. The motion made her dizzy. "Over there, somewhere."

Before she could say it, Hazel was out of the car, the gun in her hand.

Carina was out too. She reached out for Hazel's arm, grabbing her as tight as she could. "Hey," she said, trying to sound soft, warm, maternal. "You don't need to do . . . that. We can jog the rest of the way. That's our best shot. Leave Larry to his corn."

From somewhere, out in the field, they heard a car door slam.

Hazel shook her head. "Do you think he's going to let *us* leave?"

And then, as if on cue, they heard the roar of Larry Dell. "Where are you?" he screamed. "Where the fuck are you?"

Carina loosened her grip when she heard the rustling of the corn. The sky was pink with twilight and they were not alone.

Chapter Twenty-Six

REALLY, CARINA WAS just following Hazel.

She didn't see it as such a sin, really. Why not follow the girl? She had the gun, didn't she? She was prepared to use it, wasn't she?

Yes, yes she was. She knew that she was. She called out into the corn, "Larry! Larry! I want to talk to you about my schedule!" She cackled as she said it. She waved the gun around, theatrically.

She's sixteen years old, Carina remembered. This was as much for Larry as it was for her. She could still see the road from where they were—the corn had been smashed down and twisted underneath their vehicle. "Hazel, we can still leave. We can get out of here."

"No, not yet." She had the gun pointed to the sky, like an action hero she probably saw in the movies. She looked small next to the corn, she looked like she was fading from view in the magic hour twilight.

"It's getting late," said Carina. "I don't want to die," she said more feebly.

"Neither does Larry!" Hazel screamed. Her voice quaked when she yelled.

Carina felt her stomach drop to her knees.

We're going to die out here, aren't we?

Hazel ventured onward and Carina, realizing that the gun did not age her, did not protect her from herself, followed.

They disappeared between corn stalks taller than them. The sky was on fire. On a different day, it would have been beautiful. A wind picked up and everything around them shook with the insistent warning of a rattlesnake's tail. Carina gasped. Her hands dropped to her side. She blinked.

No, not now.

But yes, yes now.

Her heart beat in her ears. She heard it tapping sixteenth notes, and as soon as she heard it, they doubled in speed. Her heart was a jackhammer. Her fingers were feeling numb. Parts of her face felt like they were losing blood. The world turned around her and she lifted her arm to her head to try and find some sort of balance, some sort of center to the world. She breathed quickly. She was going to hyperventilate.

Suddenly, the cornfield was the supermarket, her old apartment, her bed in the farmhouse—and she felt her uselessness more acutely than ever—as Hazel vanished from her sight.

Larry Dell was the king of Greentree. He was its richest man, most diversified, most *seen*. He was the Lancelot of the Knights of Commerce—the highest ranking position, a director. Of sorts. He had managed to turn a dying industry, one that he had a great amount of passion for as a young boy, into a thriving business. The small town video store—like cockroaches, a survivor of all disasters.

There was no leaving Greentree for Larry Dell. He was a businessman, a natural elitist—and he saw no way in Hell that the ship needed to go down. Obviously, whatever lived out here had reneged on its bargain. Well, fine. Bargains can be renegotiated. If all the other bastards in town wanted to spend an eternity in nerve-searing agony, they could be his guest. Larry was willing to talk.

These things spoke in blood, didn't they? They were spirits, entities of the earth, right?

Well, maybe more blood was the answer. If one wasn't enough, maybe two would be.

And as Larry crept low to the ground, listening intently, he wondered if those spirits were listening to his thoughts. His hands scrambled in the dirt, seeking a weapon—any weapon—with which to do the killing (*and maybe that was it!* He *needed to do the killing this time!*) and came up with an old buck knife, coated in hardened mud and rust.

It was as if a prayer was being answered.

He listened for the girl and was met with an answer.

Carina could not stand any longer.

The ground came to meet her face, swift and cold and hard. She'd never fainted before. This time, no one came to save her. There was no rushing feet, no "poor dears." It was just the corn and the wind and the sound of a dozen heavy footsteps.

Make it stop, she told her heart.

Stop being scared, she told her brain.

Get the fuck up, she told her body.

WE, THE MANY, WILL PURGE OUR LANDS OF THOSE THAT KEEP US UNDER THEIR THUMBS. WHAT COMMUNITY IS TRULY A COMMUNITY WHEN IT IS BUILT ON THE BACKS OF OTHERS? WHICH OF US FARMS THE FIELDS? WHICH OF US BRINGS BLOOD TO THESE SOILS? TO THOSE THAT ARE SO RESOLUTE IN THEIR SUPERIORITY—WE OFFER AN ALTERNATIVE TO THEIR STATION.

THIS ALTERNATIVE IS DEATH. BY OUR HANDS, BY THOSE THAT YOU HAVE SUBJUGATED FOR SO LONG.

IT IS TRUE, WE ARE NOT WORLDLY. BUT THAT DOES NOT MAKE US WEAK. WE CAN BE FOOLED, AS OUR RULERS HAVE SEEN IN THE PAST. BUT SILVER TONGUES RUN RED WITH RIGHTEOUS VIOLENCE WHEN THE TIME IS RIGHT.

THE CLOCK IS STRIKING TWELVE, LARRY DELL—YOUR TIME IS UP.

Hazel's rage made her see Larry in every shadow. And in the corn, there were many shadows. A twig snapping sent her barrel in one direction; a rustling of leaves sent her crosshairs on a wilted stalk. She didn't know how many bullets were left in her father's pistol, but she only needed one to kill Larry.

She couldn't walk softly, not in her boots. She stomped and thrashed through the corn.

Her mother, dead—immortalized as porn for sickos. Her

father—a guilt-ridden shell of himself, doomed to an eternity of agony. And she herself—a teenage orphan, a future runaway.

No, she wouldn't go quietly.

"Larry! Come out, you piece of shit! Get the fuck out of the corn! Stop hiding, Larry! I've come to kill you!"

When she couldn't find him, when her rage didn't act as the magnet she wished it too, she ran forward, running through the dead crops, snapping stalks in her wake. "Come here!" she screamed. "Where are you?" she sobbed. The night had come quietly, like a great cat stalking its prey, and in the darkness of the night, she swung the pistol once more, an act of futility, when she recognized breathing.

Closer, he thought.

Get up!

CRUNCH!

Hazel spun around and the gun snapped with recoil when she pulled the trigger. In a single flash, she saw the humanoids walking toward her. One strobe and she could make out their faces of burlap and straw. There were so many of them, so many endless toilers. She screamed. She screamed again. Her throat was raw from all the screaming and she realized suddenly that *these were the things* that killed her mother.

She lifted the pistol. It was too dim to see but she could hear their crunching footsteps. They were getting closer, they were getting so close—

Fuck.

Hazel yelped in surprise.

She buckled. Searing pain.

She tried grabbing for her heel, where the knife had entered. Blood oozed from the wound, crawling through her fingers. Hazel cried out, aware of two things: that the scarecrows were coming, and Larry Dell was now climbing on top of her body.

Her hand reached for the gun.

Carina heard the gunshot, then heard another. The bullet went whizzing through the corn, sending soft pops as it tagged leaves on its trajectory. She was doing what they always told her to do: to breathe, to count, to go to another place, to recognize her triggers, and practice mindfulness. And as she did those things—the things she was supposed to do—she found herself stabilizing. When she opened her eyes, the world was pitch black.

But, she stood up.

She breathed in a lungful of cool air.

She started forward. "Hazel! Hazel!"

Her heart was pounding, but it was a regular pounding, an *I'm-scared-as-shit* pounding.

Another gunshot. A flash of light, close to the ground. It was so loud it hurt. She put her hand to her ear.

To the right, a little further.

Two explosions. Ears ringing. The smell of gunpowder hung in the air.

"Oh fuck," said a tiny voice, the voice of a child.

She couldn't see what was happening, but she could hear the voice of a man screaming.

"Fuck you!" he said, indignant. "Fuck all of you!"

And then, in the dark—silence.

"Hazel?" she whispered.

There was an answer, albeit weak: a whimper. She crouched down and felt for Hazel, crawling on hands and knees. "Are you okay? I can't see. Where are you? Let me help . . . "

Her hands rummaged in the cold earth until they came across Hazel's cold body—small and wet, soaked through with blood. When Carina's hands touched her, the girl's body jerked.

"No," Hazel whispered. "That hurts."

Wherever she touched her hurt. Hazel's tiny body quivered in the blackness, her body had been cut to pieces. Puncture wounds littered her flesh and she cried out into the night for her mother.

"Mom, Mom," she whined.

Carina cried. She didn't know what else to do.

"Wait," said the girl.

And Carina held her head down to her body, putting her ear to her blood.

It was the familiar sound of footsteps. Many of them.

Her body tensed and she thought right then of yelling. *Take me! Do it! End it!*

But Hazel, even in her weakness, answered her thoughts. "They don't care about us. It's theirs now. They're done."

Her muscles were all locked up, hard as rocks, as she felt them pass her, their ancient, greasy clothing rubbing against her skin. Their burlap on her cheeks. The itchiness of their straw against her body. She gasped, feeling them pass.

"They don't care," mumbled Hazel. "About us. They don't care. Carina?"

"Yes, Hazel?" When those beings passed, going to their work in the corn, Carina knelt down again beside Hazel's body.

"Don't let me die here. Take me somewhere else."

"Don't say that," said Carina, wiping tears from her eyes.

"Just take me somewhere."

Carina tried to ignore the request. "Where's Larry?" she asked.

There was a pause, a small cough. But Carina could feel the girl smile in the darkness. "He's everywhere," she said, with a painful chuckle.

Carina gathered the girl in her arms. She held the girl easily. She was stronger than she thought.

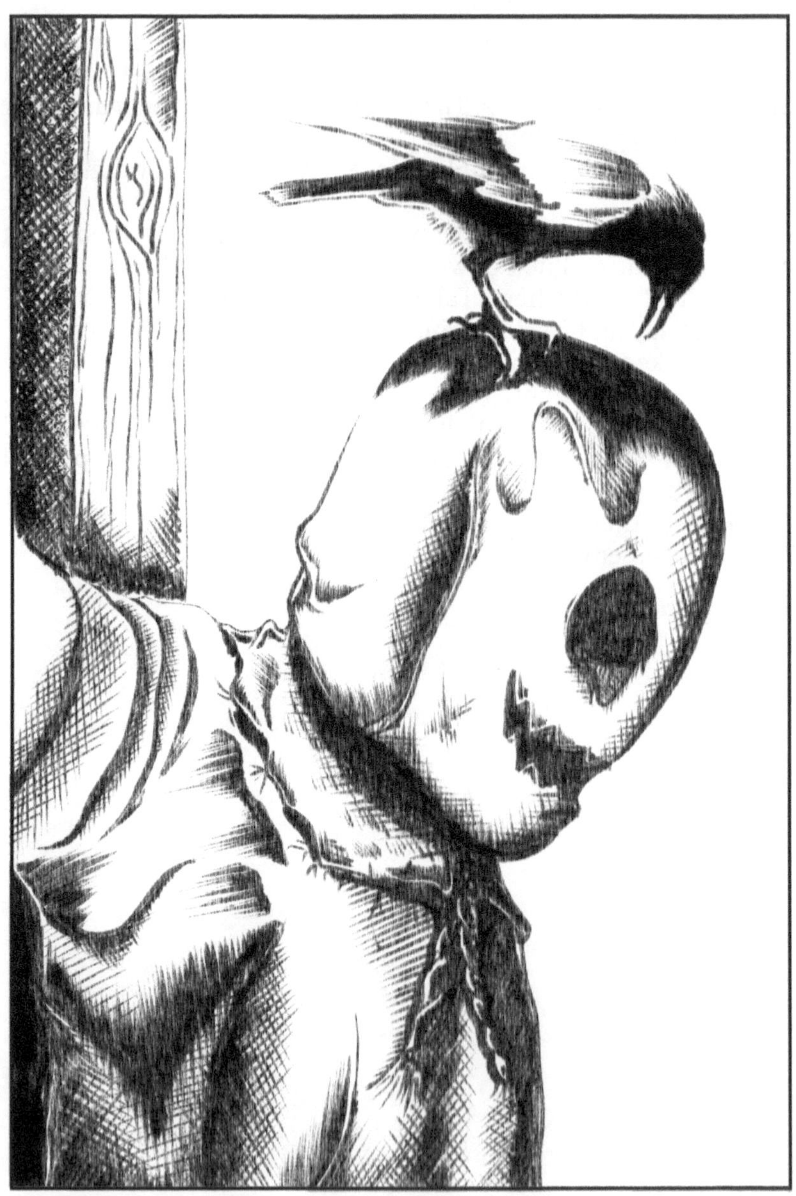

Chapter Twenty-Seven

By THE TIME she passed those tall pines, she ached. But somehow, she knew she could walk miles more, continents if needed.

Past the sky-tall pines, and then further still. Greentree was behind them.

Hazel died in the grass, under a sky full of brilliant stars. The last thing she said was "Thank you."

Carina collapsed, under those same stars, hugging her body tight. In a way, it was an apology. Or a eulogy.

Frost bit Carina's body as morning came. She couldn't let go of Hazel until sunrise.

CHAPTER TWENTY-EIGHT

CARINA WENT BACK with the morning light. She didn't know why exactly.

Sure, there were things to pick up from her homestead, but these things were not important things. She could find new things, make new money. There was no reason to go back to Greentree . . . except.

In the corn, for a brief moment, she had a feeling. A familiar sensation. A presence.

She went back because she believed Hazel when she said that the things in the field did not care about them, that their work was done. She didn't know why they didn't care about them, but she reckoned that they had their reasons. Maybe she and Hazel were too pathetic to care about. A woman and a child.

A dead child.

The walk was harder without Hazel. She would've preferred to feel her weight in her arms.

When she arrived back into town, the sun was high in the morning sky and the air was cool. The corn glinted gold. She saw the bed and breakfast ahead, but just before it, she saw the cars that ran off the road the night prior. Emily's old car, Larry's SUV, buried deep in the corn.

She sniffed. The specifics of the night had vanished from her memory. She could remember the broad strokes, as if she were a spectator. *Hazel went out looking for Larry. He stabbed her. The things tore him apart.*

With a chill, she noticed that the posts in the field were empty.

I wonder where they went?

She felt something calling to her in the corn and one step after the other led her back to where last night her friend had been killed.

Where am I being led? she wondered.

But her steps did the work. They led her on, deep into the golden corn where now, for once, she felt some delight.

The presence she felt grew stronger. It was like a magnet, leading her to true north.

Deep in the corn, bathed in its essence, she was close to the house. She could see its roof over the swaying stalks.

When she found him, mangled at her feet, a weight lifted from her.

"Here lies the body of Steve Calico," she said, to no one.

His eyes were glassy and frozen in fear. His limbs were held to his body by only a strand of sinew. His flesh was soggy and wet. Decay had set in.

There were no birds in the air.

She looked down at Steve and nodded grimly, leaving him—forever.

Acknowledgements

This book wouldn't be possible without two things: anxiety and Spirit Halloween. *Greentree* started to come together after a long streak of panic-related trips to the ER where my heart was pounding out of my chest and my doctors kept telling me that everything was fine, when everything did not feel fine *at all*. It's funny how life slithers into the stories we tell, because I didn't set out to write a story about anxiety, I set out to write a story about killer scarecrows.

Walking through Halloween stores in early September, trying on masks, swishing plastic machetes, and stomping down on those STEP HERE markers that bring animatronics to herky-jerky life is a special sort of inspiration. It brings out the Monster Kid in me, the one fascinated by all manner of hungry ghouls. Near the beginning of the season, I came across a particularly fearsome looking scarecrow, and the eleven-year old inside me's eyes became black discs. I realized that while scarecrows were great horror iconography, they were woefully underused in actual horror media. The wheels turned and ideas started snapping into place.

Anxiety and scarecrows. I guess that's how books are written.

A lot of wonderful people helped me with this book. First off, I have to thank Christopher O'Halloran, Erik McHatton, and Joseph Andre Thomas for giving early feedback on *Greentree* and helping to shape it into the book it is today. Great first readers are hard to come by, but you all made it feel easy.

I'm lucky to call myself friends with many authors and artists who have offered their support, let me whine in their DMs, or simply been a source of ongoing inspiration. Thank you to Patrick Barb, Jolie Toomajan, TJ Price, Tim Bloom, RSL, PL McMillan, Andrew F. Sullivan, Christi Nogle, Ai Jiang, Ivy Grimes, Michael Boulerice, Caleb Stephens, Emma E. Murray, Danger Slater, Matt Brandenburg, Jon Padgett, Curtis Ghoul, and so many more. I treasure every one of you.

Thank you to Stefan Koidl for the jaw-dropping art. I couldn't imagine a better cover.

I'd like to thank my wife, Sarah, for continually being my best friend and rock solid support system as I suffer the ups and downs of an absurd hobby that brings me to the highest highs and lowest lows. Seriously, I couldn't do any of this without you.

Finally, this book wouldn't even be in your hands if it weren't for the team from Tenebrous Press. Matt and Alex, you have done so much for me, and thanks will never be enough.

Content Warnings

Being a work of mature Horror, a degree of violence, gore, sex and/or death is to be expected.

In addition, **A Spectre is Haunting Greentree** contains scenes of *Domestic Violence* and *Child Death*.

Please be advised.

About the Contributors

Carson Winter is an award-winning author, punker, and raw nerve. His short fiction has been featured in *Apex, Vastarien*, and *Tales to Terrify*. His novels and novellas have been published by **Tenebrous Press** and **Apocalypse Party**. He lives in the Pacific Northwest.

Stefan Koidl is an illustrator and Krampus mask carver who hails from Austria.

Matt Blairstone (he/him) is a writer, editor, artist, indie comics creator and the publisher/founder of **Tenebrous Press**. He lives in Portland, Oregon. Sleep is folly.

TENEBROUS PRESS

aims to drag the malleable Horror genre into newer, Weirder territory with stories that are incisive, provocative, intelligent and terrifying; delivered by voices diverse and unsung.

NEW WEIRD HORROR

FIND OUT MORE:

www.tenebrouspress.com
Social Media @TenebrousPress